What Peop

When is Tomorr... ...ate look at a caregiver's journey dealing with dementia. Nancy Seiling's book comes in satisfying, bite-size morsels, accompanied by a philosophical look at each interaction, and a prayer to bring insight and resolution.

Through it all, runs the gift of liberating laughter that often brings relief, changed situations, and attitudes. This is a true gift to caregivers and loved ones, as well. As I read, I found myself wishing I was born a Dubrick—then I realized I could nurture and grow the gift of laughter in myself—what a precious take-away. This book will surely bring comfort, insight, and support to many, especially to caregivers.

Ruth Meyer
Author, Inspirational Speaker, Caregiver

With humbleness and plenty of good humour, Seiling wraps her arms around the reader and takes you on a journey of dementia with her beloved mother. She offers such good practical advice on every page, always turning to her great and wonderful God for comfort, hope, strength, and forgiveness.

Barbara Heagy B.A., B.Ed., M.A.
Author, Dancer, Retired Teacher

Nancy Seiling has written a wonderful devotional and I thoroughly enjoyed reading her stories and uplifting prayers.

In this devotional Nancy stands with those who are battling and assures them that they are not alone. Her delightful sense of humour, words of wisdom, and heart of encouragement will be an absolute blessing to her readers.

Dr Shelley Torcetti

Author, HIV/AIDS Researcher

Nancy's devotional provides us with an exemplary picture of the joys and grief, the satisfaction and weariness, and all the ups and downs that come with caregiving.

In *When Is Tomorrow? A Devotional for Caregivers,* Nancy shows us how to be God with skin on; how she was able to bring God's memories to her mom and to others going through the long, frightening, neurological deterioration we call dementia. I highly recommend this devotional for all caregivers who desire to faithfully live in the memories of God with their loved ones.

Paul Shrier, Ph.D

Professor of Practical Theology
Azusa Pacific University

Through the author's personal experiences, she has created a beautiful devotional for caregivers and their families!

Theresa Goldrick

Avid Reader, Book Reviewer and DSW

May these stories cause you to laugh, inspire you & even shed a tear or two. Our God is faithful. You are not alone.

Nancy Sieling

When Is Tomorrow?

A Devotional for Caregivers

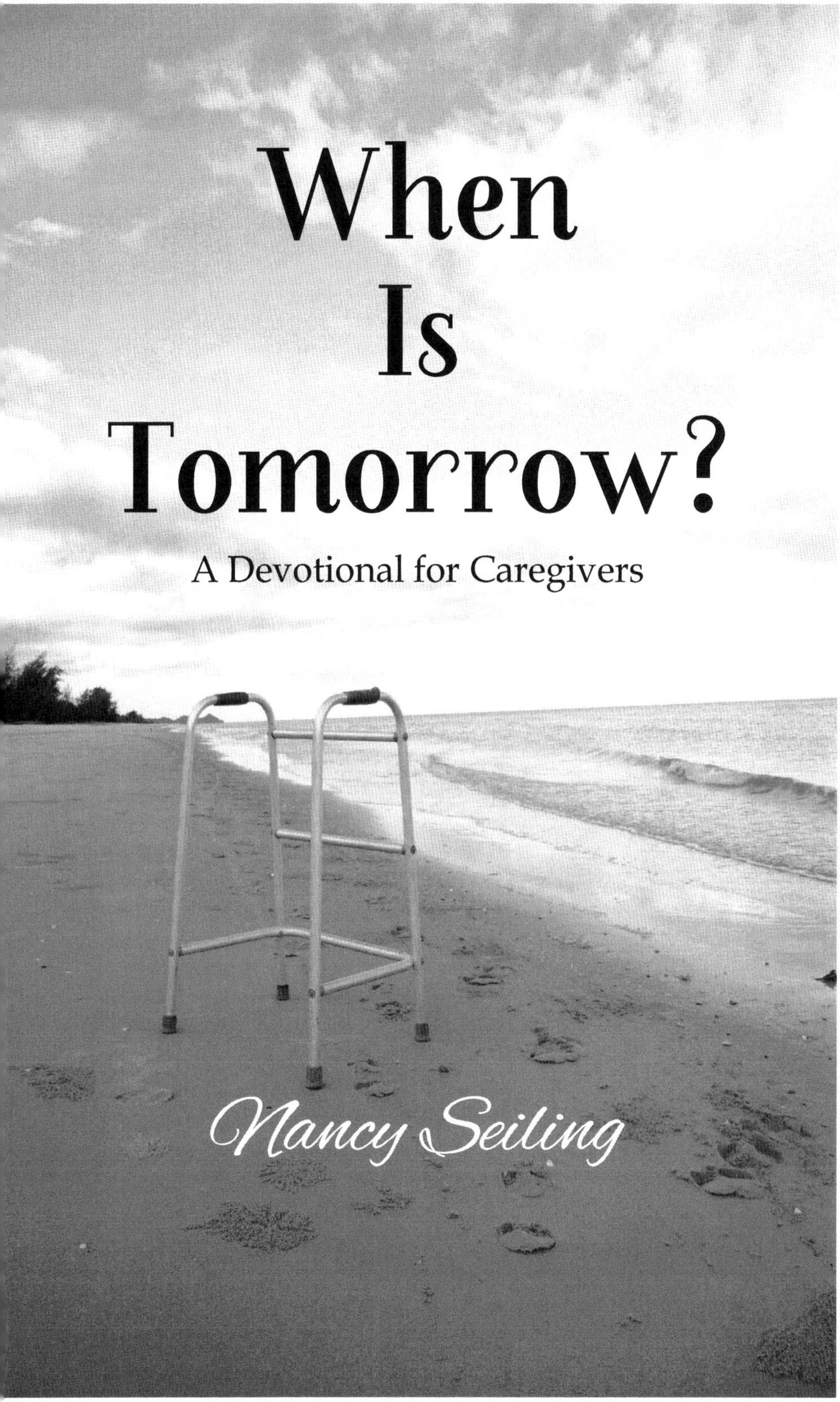
When Is Tomorrow?
A Devotional for Caregivers
Nancy Seiling

When is Tomorrow?

First Edition.
ISBN: 978-1-988155-22-7

Cover Design by Amanda Belec
@thirteen13designz

Angel Hope Publishing
www.glynisbelec.com

Printed in Canada
Innovative Print
innovativeprint.ca

Cover Images: Lightstock.com & Deposit Photos
Back cover photo: Queintin Tang

To the compassionate and caring staff
at St. Jacobs Place and Heritage House.
You are an amazing team.

Table of Contents:

Foreword i
Introduction iii
Doctor's Visit 1
Blue Housecoat 3
The Best Medicine 5
Difficult Decision 7
Broken Hip 10
Surgery 13
Cheese with that Whine? 15
High Goals 17
Nurse Nancy 19
Happy Birthday to Me 21
Being a Servant 24
Free at Last! 26
Stronger Every Day 28
Some Days are Tougher Than Others 31
Yellow Jackets Are Nice 34
Fun Phone 36
Anticipated Phone 38
Mom's Clothes Advice 40
Drive in the Country 42
Accidents Will Happen 44
Antidote for Depression 47
Lunch with Family 49
Death in the Family 51
Reliving Bad News 53
Appreciative Mother 56
Day Out and About 59
Digging in a Snowbank 61
Life Can Be Tough 63
Not the Way We'd Planned 65
Meltdown 68
Crisis 70

Life Happens 73
Dementia Does Strange Things 76
More Than One Birthday 79
Laughter 82
Growing Old Isn't for Sissies 85
Low Self-Esteem 88
Good Things in Our Mouths 90
A Taste of Home 93
Happy Birthday Mom 95
Noah Martin Summer Sausage 97
Thanksgiving 100
Little Things 103
Routines 105
Romance 107
Extra Special Breakfast 109
Mom Goes to RIM Park 111
Early Morning Phone Call 114
Childhood Memory 117
Hard on Myself 119
Precious Memories 121
Toothless 124
Answer on the Way 126
Mom is on Her Way to New Teeth! 128
A Very Bad, Not So Good Day 130
Another Meltdown 132
Memories 135
Mama in Quarantine 145
No Germs Through Phonelines 147
Mama is Declining 149
Change in Plans 151
Shower Curtain 154
Fruit of His Labour 156
Sad Mama 159
When is Tomorrow? 161
Tomorrow is Today! 163

When Trouble Comes 166
Difficult Times 168
Christmas 2018 170
Downhill 173
Two Moms 176
Laughter Helps 178
Interruptions 180
Compassion 183
Trouble in Paradise 185
God's Idea 188
Indoor Picnic 191
Difficult Phone Call 194
Dementia Fog 196
A Close Call 199
Everyone Has a Story 201
Excellent Advice 204
To Give or Not to Give 206
Laughing is Good 209
Wishful Thinking 211
Worried Mother 214
Wisdom 217
Cry for Help 219
Cute Mother 222
Not a Place for Old People 225
Memory Problem 228
Organized Mother 231
To God Be the Glory 233
Peace, Beautiful Peace 235
Going Back in Time 237
Sing a Song of Praise 239
Loving Heavenly Father 241
Family 243
Happy Mom 245
Niagara Falls 247
Wonderful Easter 249

Life Isn't Always Easy 251
Compliments Count 253
Tough Times 255
Meal Gone Bad 257
Changes Life Brings 259
Thank God for Good Days 261
Personal Support Workers 263
Loving Family 265
Hard to Watch Sometimes 267
In Someone Else's Shoes 269
Forgive Quickly 271
Be Kind 273
Home Is Where the Heart Is 276
But Mom! 278
Birthday Musings 280
Perfect Peace 283
Nice Birthday 285
Mama Getting Weaker 287
Safe in the Arms of Jesus 289
Epilogue 291
My Example 293
A Celebration of Life 295
Acknowledgements 299
About the Author 301

Foreword

I dab away a tear as I listen to the words of the song, "Long Road[1]." The haunting lyrics are a near-perfect description of my caregiver journey as I walked alongside my husband through a decade-long struggle with dementia. The male trio, Reborn, sing about the *long road* as being one with twists and turns where it may feel as if there's a hurricane or you're climbing a mountain; a road where it's difficult to put one foot in front of the other, where even the strongest feel like giving up.

The song leads me to Nancy's devotional book, *When is Tomorrow? A Devotional for Caregivers*. How heart-warming to read of a caregiver journey filled with dedication, determination, encouragement, laughter, and music—despite the pain of dementia.

Dementia is the umbrella term used to describe the effects on the brain caused by various diseases such as Alzheimer's, vascular disease, Lewy Body, Huntington's, Parkinson's, and others. These diseases may cause the brain's neural connections to deteriorate, to slowly die, affecting the person's ability to remember, to reason, to make decisions, and to perform tasks.

Dementia is puzzling, no two cases are alike, and it may last up to a decade. A long road indeed. Statistics tell us half a million people in Canada are affected by it, and, sadly, this number is predicted to double in the next dozen or so years[2].

To walk with someone, to be a caregiver for someone suffering from the effects of dementia, is a challenging task. The declining cognitive functions may be readily understood but the person's aberrant behavior, ranging from comical to combative, often leave caregivers scratching their heads, so to speak. Restlessness and walking away may be a common concern. The

---

1 "Long Road." Radio Version. https://youtu.be/d0xVPt6yYg8

2 Alzheimer Society, Canada. https://alzheimer.ca/

professionals refer to this as "sundowning." When dusk approaches with the setting sun, the patient becomes restless and seeks an exit by which to leave their surroundings. Statistics tell us 80% of caregivers suffer from depression and sometimes die before the patient does.[3] This may be attributed to age, but also to the stress of caregiving. The load is especially heavy for those who care for a loved one 24-7.

Reading Nancy's encouraging devotional, rekindled memories of my own journey. Caring for my Mom was much like Nancy's journey. But, despite amazing blessings, I found the cost of caring for my husband much higher, the pain of parting more severe.

The "Long Road" song ends with a plea to not give up, to not let go because, someday, looking back, we will see it was worth it all.

Nancy's sentiment for sure. And, yes, mine, also!

Angelina Fast-Vlaar.

Award-winning author of four books, including the latest, *Bring Each Other Home – a Caregiver's Journey*. www.angelinafast.com

---

[3] https://www.cbc.ca/cbcdocspov/episodes/the-caregivers-club

Introduction

I treasure my quiet time with the Lord, and that includes Bible reading and using a devotional book for my personal edification. I learn a great deal from a devotional because it helps guide my understanding of scripture and how it relates to my life. I connect well to personal stories, which is why I felt impressed to write about my mother and include them in *When is Tomorrow?*

I am the middle child of three girls. Daddy realized early that God had given him a girl's trio, so when we were young, we began singing as a family. A father and his three girls singing sweet harmony. He was happy with that. Sadly, Daddy had a massive heart attack and died at age 39, leaving my mom a young widow at 37. Because of our mother's example, we bravely carried on and decided to change our stage name from "The Dubrick Family" to "The Dubrick Sisters," and we sang together for years.

After being a widow for 10 years, Mom met Ken. They married and had a good life together for over 40 years until dementia reared its ugly head. Eventually, Ken had to be sent to a nursing home, and then slowly but surely, mom's mind also drifted into this terrible disease. For years all she wanted was to go to sleep and wake up in Heaven, but God did not answer that request right away. He kept her here on earth for a special reason, and that reason, I believe, is the book you now hold in your hand.

The last years of Mom's life were nuggets of pure gold, and I journalled the highs and lows, joys and sorrows as a caregiver. As I posted stories on social media, I was surprised at the large number of people around the world who read them. Many suggested I should write a book. I'd always come back with, "Easy for you to say!" and left it at that. Then, I met my editor (at a yard sale of all places), who also turned out to be a publisher, and so that started the process.

Too often caregivers are forgotten. People showed concern for my mother and asked how she was doing, but seldom did they ask how my sister, Janet, and I were doing as we visited and helped look after Mom every day. Perhaps this has happened to you as a caregiver.

When is Tomorrow? was written with the caregiver in mind. But it is more than that. It contains stories that I hope and pray will offer more than instruction of how to be a good caregiver. My prayer is that this devotional will make you laugh, give you a lift, allow you to cry, or just remind you that you are not alone in your struggles.

I could feel God's favour as I typed each story and knew that He guided my every step. I thank Him often for the opportunity I had to reach out and share the peaks and valleys in my own journey. My prayer is that this devotional would help as you care for others.

May God speak to you through these pages. May you understand that He is with you each and every step of the way. And may God bless you, fellow traveller, as the story of a very special woman slowly unfolds.

Mom

My mother was a "behind the scenes" person, who quietly served the God she loved, but she did not want attention. She sewed all of our matching "singing dresses." (Just to be clear, the dresses didn't sing, but they sure were pretty.) Mom wholeheartedly supported our ministry and even chose many of the songs for us to learn. She felt comfortable in that role. We often laughed at the irony of her having three daughters who all loved being on stage while she avoided the spotlight.

In 2016, our youngest sister Jane died of cancer, so that left Janet and me to care for Mom as best we could. Although neither of us could take care of our mother in our homes because of our ministries and frequent missionary trips, we faithfully visited her in the retirement home and then in the nursing home. We kept in close contact with staff and would talk to Mom on the phone often. We were as involved as we could be and understood the strain of caring for an elderly parent with dementia while looking after our own families, and undertaking our own day to day responsibilities.

Throughout our caregiving, Janet and I relied on our loving Heavenly Father to help us. He knew our situation and He knew that we could only handle a heavy load for so long. Often we were reminded of scriptures that strengthened and encouraged. I love the 23rd Psalm where it says in verses one, two, and three: "The Lord is my shepherd; I shall not want. He makes me to lie down in green pastures; He leads me beside the still waters. He restores my soul; He leads me in the paths of righteousness For His name's sake." I love the fact that the Shepherd sometimes makes us lie down in green pastures for our own good. But what does He do while we are there? "He restores my soul."

So, before a calamity happens where you are forced to take a break, schedule something that you truly love to do. You may find that a simple walk in the woods or a park or reading a good book will do wonders. Everyone is different, but it is important to have "down time." Refuse to allow guilt to take over and say it aloud if you have to, "I deserve this time away and I need it!" Sometimes speaking to myself out loud really helps and it does calm me down (although I try to stay away from others when I am doing that, lest they wonder.)

Ask the Heavenly Father what you should do to take care of yourself and then listen. He is such a creative Father and has the ideal solution that will give you the best rest and refreshment. Follow up on it, and you'll be pleasantly surprised at the difference it will make.

I learned much while caring for my mother. Now I want to pass it on. Ready to turn the page in *When is Tomorrow?* My prayer is that you find encouragement for your journey as you do.

Doctor's Visit

Do not sorrow, for the joy of the Lord is your strength.
Nehemiah 8:10b

I had an interesting morning with Mom at the doctor's office. As part of the examination, the doctor gave her a memory test. Poor Mom didn't know what city we were in, what day or month or the year it was, but when the doctor asked, "What country do you live in?" Mom brightened and said, "That's easy. It's Canada. I know because Nancy and I were talking on the way here about how much we love Canada." Then I jumped in and said, "And we even sang O Canada in the car."

The doctor was a delightful woman. She actually got a little misty-eyed and said, "Oh, that is so sweet!" After the appointment, Mom was tired, so I took her back to St. Jacobs Place where she lived. As I was getting her ready for her nap, she let out a little burp and laughed. I told her the story of when my daughter-in-law Sarah was putting our 4-year-old grandson, Trenton, to bed one afternoon. He suddenly blurted out, "I tooted."

"Congratulations," Sarah said.

Trenton, in all his innocence, said, "Why congratulations? I didn't even practice!"

Mom thought that was funny and then proceeded to burp a second time.

"And unlike Trenton, I practiced!" We both laughed.

My family never knew what Mom was going to come up with next, but one thing for sure, she always kept us laughing.

Lighten Up

Although many situations aren't necessarily funny, sometimes, as caregivers, we have to dig a little deeper to find the humour. Most of the time, it's well worth the effort. Laughter reduces stress and that is a fitting goal.

Talking to God

Lord, there are times when the load is so heavy that I can't even smile. However, I ask that You reveal to me the little nuggets of joy that I would normally miss. You said in Your word that joy will give me strength. I need this joy right now. Thank You for the gift of laughter. Amen.

Blue Housecoat

Anxiety in the heart of man causes depression,
But a good word makes it glad.
Proverbs 12:25

My sisters and I often wondered why Mom disliked attention from anyone other than family. Her desire to keep in the background and not draw attention to herself puzzled us, and no amount of prodding could get her to tell us why she felt this way. One incident, however, gave us a glimpse into her thought process.

Years ago, Ken bought Mom a beautiful housecoat and she treasured it. The teal colour, along with the soft, shimmering fabric that flowed down to the floor, added to the charm. She hardly ever wore it though. She made it clear she would only wear it if she had to go to the hospital. So it always looked brand new.

One day, Mom had a change of heart.

"To heck with it," Mom said. "I'm going to start wearing this housecoat all the time."

And she did. One evening, she had it on when a nurse came to her door to check on her. Next day Mom told us what happened.

"When that nurse came in, she kept staring at my housecoat," Mom said, "and I knew that she was thinking, 'Who does Flo Kufske think she is, wearing such a fancy housecoat?'"

This shocked us a bit. I said, "Mom, the nurse was probably thinking she had never seen such a lovely housecoat before and was admiring it."

That seemed to sink in and caused Mom to feel differently. She proudly wore it from then on and didn't mind who saw it.

That incident revealed how Mom's dislike for undue attention was fueled by the feeling she was being judged. It seemed, to her, that if someone was looking at her, it was with disdain. Perhaps her hair wasn't good enough; could she have been wearing the wrong clothes? Maybe she felt others were thinking she was doing something improper, and on and on. No wonder she did not like attention if she thought it was always negative. Our poor mama.

Our Words Count

We may not be aware of the impact of our words, especially on the vulnerable. Each of us has had something spoken over us in the past that has either lifted us up or dragged us down and it turned into a defining moment in our lives. There is an adage that says, "Sticks and stones may break my bones, but words will never hurt me." That statement is simply not true. Words can be a powerful tool to either use positively or negatively. Let us work hard to make sure our words are uplifting, for it will make a difference to the ones we care for.

Talking to God

Oh God. You alone know the damage that has been done by careless, mean-spirited words in my life and in the lives of others. Even though I am not responsible for what others say to me or about me, I am responsible for what I say to others. Put a guard over my mouth and compassion in my heart so only good things come out. If I don't have anything positive to say, may I simply shut up! Amen.

The Best Medicine

And let the peace of God rule in your hearts, to which also you were called in one body; and be thankful.
Colossians 3:15

We were very happy that Mom got along well with her female doctor, so it wasn't usually a problem to get her to an appointment when she needed one. The doctor got a real kick out of Mom and there was always a lot of laughter coming from the exam room. Because I stayed with her, I had a jolly good time right along with them.

For one visit though, Mom seemed uptight. The nurse handed Mom a sterile container and asked for a urine sample before her appointment with the doctor. Mom went into the bathroom but a few minutes later, came out with an empty container. She apologized, but the doctor didn't seem overly concerned.

"No problem. You can try again later."

Mom had a rash on her buttocks. The doctor prescribed a cream and then she moved on to checking her ears. Her doctor noticed there was a wax buildup, so she asked a nurse to flush them out. All this time we were laughing at one thing and then another.

After we left the room, Mom proudly said, "Well, I've had my rear and my ear checked so now I'm good to go!" Much laughter by all the staff. Then the doctor suggested she try to give a urine sample again, and this time Mom came out with the container filled to the brim. With a huge grin on her face, she proudly announced, "And I could have given a whole lot more too!" This time even those in the waiting room laughed.

I think we should have sold tickets for the entertainment.

Good Times Can Happen Anytime

Many older people, especially if they are suffering from dementia, can be fearful of doctors for various reasons. It is important to remain calm at all times and just go along with whatever mood they are in. If there is any chance of laughter, go for it, for there is something relaxing about a laugh or even a smile.

Talking to God

Oh Father. There are many things that make me anxious, but those who suffer from mental or emotional problems are so much more susceptible than I am. I understand that, even though it is hard to deal with sometimes. Teach me to trust You and show me how to respond to the one I care for, so whatever the situation is, it can go smoothly. Amen.

Difficult Decision

Draw near to God and He will draw near to you.
James 4:8

Before moving to St. Jacobs, Mom and Ken had loved living in their little condo near Rockway Gardens in Kitchener. They could see the finely groomed gardens from their living room window and often walked over to enjoy the gloriously inviting colourful flowers, the fountains, and the delightful bridges dotting the grounds.

Mom and Ken had happily lived there for 25 years, but when they both began showing signs of dementia, we knew something had to be done. Mom could no longer cook, so, although it wasn't easy, my sisters and I helped them see the wisdom of moving into a retirement home. The one we all liked best was a five-star establishment in the little town of St. Jacobs. The suite was lovely and the food, we discovered, was excellent. Plus, there were many places to walk, and since that was one of their favourite pastimes, this suited them perfectly.

All was arranged. They settled in well and never regretted the move to St. Jacobs. Things went well for about three years, until Ken's dementia became serious enough that it caused Mom much anxiety. Because of all the stress and her weakened immune system, she ended up with shingles.

We knew something had to be done. My sisters and I, along with Ken's two sons and daughters-in-law, talked about it and eventually made the difficult decision to move Ken to a nursing home. The only one with an available bed was a little further than we had hoped, but we promised Mom that we'd take her there often to visit.

Plans were put in place and before we knew it, Ken was settling into the nursing home routine. Janet, Jane, and I faithfully took turns honouring our commitment, and it worked out well. It didn't take long before Mom healed from her bout of shingles and was content, especially when she knew she could visit Ken often.

We realized Mom no longer needed the larger, more expensive suite, so when a cute little room opened up on the first floor with a terrific view (views are important in our family), we moved her down and she was as happy as happy could be. She and I would often walk together. I have fond memories of those times, and she loved coming to our homes for a visit now and again. She was content to go back to her room in St. Jacobs where she felt so much at home. After a few weeks, a room opened up for Ken at the long-term care home across the river from the retirement home in St. Jacobs. Mom could walk over to visit whenever she wanted. It was perfect. My sisters and I often joined Mom for lunch at St. Jacobs Place and Mom would be thrilled whenever we did. Life was good and we were happy. This lasted about two years. Thankfully, at the time, we didn't know what lay around the corner.

Be Thankful

No matter what life throws at us, it is important to be thankful. I love this quote by Chrissy Metz. "There is something that happens when we are grateful: You continue to receive blessings." I have found this to be so true in our lives. "A thankful heart is a happy heart," so says Madame Blueberry in Veggie Tales. Remember, even on those hard days, there is always something to be thankful for, no matter how small. Try looking for something and you'll see what I mean.

Talking to God

Lord, You give me so much each day that it's easy to take things for granted. You cause the sun to rise each morning. You chase away the darkness. I am blessed as I gaze upon blue skies, fluffy clouds, green trees, and grass in the summer, and pristine sparkling snow in the winter. Even at night the moon and stars shine, so I can gaze with wonder. Help me look beyond my own problems and see all the good things and to be thankful. Amen.

Broken Hip

Trust in Him at all times, you people; Pour out your heart before Him; God is a refuge for us.
Psalm 62:8

From My Journal: June 2017

My poor Mama fell and broke her hip and needs a hip replacement. It happened quickly. She was taken to the hospital by ambulance last evening and Janet was with her. I don't drive at night, so I arrived at the hospital at 7:30 a.m. the next day and didn't arrive home until after 8:00 p.m.

It was a long day, but I'm so glad Janet and I could be there for our precious mother. My first shock when I arrived at her room was seeing that Mom's roommate was a man. Oh my. Things have changed since I was in the hospital. Mom wasn't bothered by it though and he seemed like a nice sort of guy and we got along fine. At first, Mom wanted to talk about Heaven and so we did. We even sang some choruses about Heaven, which was a little bit of Heaven in itself.

Through the curtains a little later on, I heard her roommate say to the nurse, "Those two are going to Heaven," to which the nurse replied, "Well I hope I am too!" That made us chuckle.

Later, when the nurse finished taking Mom's vital signs, she asked if she wanted the light above her bed on or off.

Mom replied, "Off, I think, 'cause I look better in the dark." The nurse got a kick out of that.

Later, I was able to go down with Mom for her chest X-ray and the doctor who had to evaluate her for surgery gave her the thumbs up.

"Do you have any trouble going pee?" he asked.

"That's what got me into this problem in the first place!" Mom said. The doctor laughed. "Yesterday, I was out with my sister and had to go potty so bad that I jumped out of the car and did a face plant."

After things settled down, when Mom was in a bit of pain, she said, "Oh horse buns!"
I'd never heard that one before.

Later, she became confused and thought she was in her own room. She was bound and determined to sit on her couch. I hurried to her side.

"Mom, you can't get out of bed."

"Well, why not?"

I calmly said, "Because you broke your hip and you're in the hospital."

*I could see her eyes come into focus as the reality of the situation became clear and she then said, "Well, I'm going to say it ... Oh horse sh**!"*

It felt good to laugh because we never heard Mom swear before. Soon she joined in with the laughter.

The surgeon had stopped in early in the afternoon to say Mom's surgery was booked, but that he kept getting bumped with emergency cases coming in and there was little he could do. We were disappointed when we realized it wouldn't happen today, but he assured us it would happen first thing tomorrow. We truly hoped it would.

This is hard on all of us.

Trials

Some days are full of great hardship. However, we need to remember to be thankful for our hospitals and the medical teams who help by using great skill and kindness. We live in a country with terrific health care and professionals who are well-trained to fix what is broken. Remembering everyone involved in caring for our loved one, reminds us of how blessed we are.

Talking to God

Oh God, who knows all things, You see me on my dark days. You have graciously provided assistance for me and I want to always remember to thank You. Please help me to not look on the dark side, but always on the bright side, because it's always there. Amen.

____

____

____

____

____

Surgery

"For My thoughts are not your thoughts, Nor are your ways My ways," says the Lord. "For as the heavens are higher than the earth, So are My ways higher than your ways, And My thoughts than your thoughts."
Isaiah 55:8-9

Mom had her hip replacement surgery and came through with flying colours. Janet was there when she was wheeled back to her room and I came later. Of course, she slept a lot, but when she woke up at 2:30, she made her needs known immediately.

"I'm hungry."

Janet and I went to the patient kitchen to see what we could find for Mom to eat. We managed to scrounge an egg salad sandwich, some ginger-ale, and a muffin for her. She ate half the sandwich, drank some ginger-ale, and took sips of water. Then announced that she felt stuffed. We tried to get her to eat supper a few hours later, but she wasn't interested so we didn't push it. Her spirits were good and it wasn't long before she kept telling Janet and me to go home. What an improvement. We were truly thankful.

I knew I would sleep better knowing Mom's surgery was over and all was well. It had been a ride for sure, but our hearts were full of thanksgiving for good surgeons, great hospitals, and terrific nurses.

I had the early shift with Mom the next day. Janet would be taking mid-afternoon and early evening. Caregivers unite!

Hospitals

Although not many people enjoy being in the hospital, it certainly is the best place to be when we need medical care. It is important to be kind and understanding of the nurses and Personal Support Workers for they have a tough job. It doesn't take much to thank staff members for all they do. Most of the time, the staff likes when family or caregivers help whenever possible in the hospital setting. It helps them and it helps you too.

Talking to God

God, I have so much to be thankful for. Although I may not understand why accidents happen, I do know, though, that You are there with me every step of the journey. Thank You for your peace and for giving me the knowledge that You are God Almighty. How I praise You. Amen.

Cheese with that Whine?

Set your mind on things above, not on things on the earth.
Colossians 3:2

On my way to the hospital to visit Mom, I heard a thunderous boom followed by the loudest noise I could imagine. I had been slowly driving through construction, thinking something big must have collided with something equally as big. The sound was deafening. It made me jump and take my foot off the gas. I frantically peered around but nothing looked out of the ordinary. So I sped up and as I pressed my foot on the accelerator, I was horrified. The dreadful noise was coming from my car!

I was aware mufflers did something, but I never knew they kept THAT much noise muffled! I sure do now. I hated to press on the gas pedal and prayed that a policeman wouldn't stop me for disturbing the peace. I figured if I was to get pulled over, I'd sob and sob. This seemed to be the last straw.

Thankfully no boys or girls in blue stopped me. I made it safely to the hospital but was mortified at how extra loud my car sounded in the parking garage. Of course, it so happened that I had to go to the fifth level because the lower levels were filled to the brim. The sound amplified and on every parking level the muffler seemed to get louder with the sound bouncing off the walls. Oh, the embarrassment of it all.

Once I arrived in Mom's room, I hugged her and then Janet and I got each other caught up to speed about what was happening with Mom. After Janet left, I called David who called our garage and they agreed to have a loaner vehicle ready for me when I got there after closing time. All I had to do was drop my keys off in the slot in the office door and drive away in a quiet car. What a relief.

I was pleased to see Mom no longer had intravenous, oxygen, or a catheter, and it was also good to see she had been up with the therapist again. I assisted Mom with supper, got her settled, and sheepishly left with my noisy car and picked up the loaner. Now, I not only had to remember where I parked in the parking garage tomorrow, but I had to remember what the loaner car looked like.

Life got harder 'n harder, but I was doing it with a smile and a song!

Insult to Injury

It often seems as if trouble comes in pairs or even threes. When we think things can't get worse, something else blindsides us and we are bewildered. The important thing, when we are feeling bogged down as caregivers, is to simply take it in stride, knowing that we are not alone in our struggles. Our situations are not all that unique. Many travel the same path. Gives a kind of special peace just knowing that.

Talking to God

Jesus said that I would have troubles, and He was telling me the truth. I am not immune from having problems. No one is and no one has a perfect life, but You are with me, Lord. I feel it. You strengthen me and help me carry on and for that, I am thankful. Amen.

High Goals

The Lord God is my strength; He will make my feet like deer's feet, And He will make me walk on my high hills.
Habakkuk 3:19

Some days it seems there aren't enough hours to accomplish the tasks at hand, while other days I wonder if the second hand on the clock has taken a holiday. How can that be?

It was one of those days. Janet had taken the morning shift. Mom was sleeping when I arrived. As I sat by her bed, I wondered how I was going to make it through the next 6 hours. I had a little pity party for myself (no one else was invited) but at least I had a good book to read.

Soon Mom woke up and needed to go to the bathroom. Believe me, it was always quite a chore to get her there. The last time Mom had to go to the bathroom, I helped her to sit on the edge of the bed. The nurse applauded our efforts. I wouldn't think of doing anything more, because I wanted her better, not flat on the floor.

It took two nurses to get Mom up and walking. She was exhausted after the ordeal. I was exhausted just watching! She did say, (many times) "I'm so spoiled at St. Jacobs Place because I can go potty anytime I want to." The hospital nurses were good though, and they just smiled.

Later, we did the bed exercises like the physical therapist showed us. Mom never complained about having to do them—even when they hurt. She's a trooper for sure!

"I want to get better, so I can go potty whenever I want to!"

Some may attain to higher goals, but you gotta love my mother for claiming this one!

The Little Things

We take our good health so much for granted, don't we? It is only when it is taken away that we fully appreciate it. Being thankful for the insignificant or the little things that keep us happy, is a good thing. As you care for your loved one today, it might be a good time to thank God for something small and see if it doesn't make you smile.

Talking to God

I have blessings all around me, but sadly, too often I take them for granted. Please remind me to open my eyes, look up and be filled with thanksgiving for all Your goodness. Amen.

Nurse Nancy

Therefore humble yourselves under the mighty hand of God, that He may exalt you in due time, casting all your care upon Him, for He cares for you.
1 Peter 5:6-7

You can call me "Nurse Nancy" from now on. I started assisting Mom in and out of bed for bathroom breaks twice, and she was still kicking. No falls. Before I even dared try, I asked her nurse how much I could do without being on the receiving end of their wrath, or worse, hurting mom.

"You've seen us do it enough times," the nurse laughed and said. "You'll do fine. Just ring if you feel you can't handle it!"

Well, I'm telling you, I'm very proud of myself because together we did it. Do I hear any "Good girl" affirmations out there?

Saturday was normally the day David and I went to yard sales, but of course, Mom came first. That said, because traffic was lighter that day, I had plenty of time before I had to be at the hospital and spotted two yard sales on the way. So, I stopped. I found a lovely journal for myself, a gift for one of my granddaughters, and a gift for one of my grandsons—all brand new and still in the box. I was thrilled! It felt like a blessing from God and I accepted His love.

There was a lovely lady in the other hospital bed in Mom's room so of course we got talking. She seemed interested in my life, so I mentioned that our whole family were ventriloquists. Her husband found out and later begged me to bring my ventriloquist doll, Jerry, in as he wanted to see a show. I didn't normally do that, but I knew it would cheer them both up. We arranged a time and my mini show was underway. They laughed and laughed. It felt good to do something to make everyone happy. I think Mom even liked it. Janet had arrived a little early to relieve me, so she got in on it, too (although she'd seen Jerry hundreds of times, so it was no big deal to her.) It was fun but I realized I was totally wiped when I walked to the car, after saying my goodbyes. I was tired and so glad to finally be home again to rest and relax—until the next time.

Times of Encouragement

God gives us little bits of encouragement during our struggles, but we don't always see them. Sometimes we get encouragement when we encourage others. He alone knows what our bodies are going through on those difficult days, and I believe, if we are in tune to His voice, He shows us how to handle things, even if it means doing something a little unusual.

Talking to God

Thank You God for Your deep interest in every aspect of my life. You long to help me, but sometimes I miss the signals and continue to try to carry my burdens alone (which is not Your plan). Give me a keen heart, open eyes, and an understanding heart to receive what You long to give me. Amen.

Happy Birthday to Me

Trust in the Lord with all your heart, And lean not on your own understanding; In all your ways acknowledge Him, And He shall direct your paths.
Proverbs 3:5-6

I must say I had a great birthday and I couldn't have been happier. David paid special attention to me before I had to leave for the early shift at the hospital to be with Mom.

When I got off the elevator, I was greeted with, "Happy Birthday Nancy," by the cleaning lady. What a nice surprise! Obviously, Mom told her it was my birthday, and she made sure to give me a happy greeting too. I really liked this cleaning lady because the first day Mom was in her room, she peeked her head through the curtains to make sure it was alright for her to clean.

"Are we playing peek-a-boo?" I asked.

She liked that and I called her my "peek-a-boo lady" from then on. She also said that Mom was very happy because she told her she was going to be released that day.

That was news to me. I hadn't heard that, so I talked to a nurse. She told me that if the therapists and doctor said it was okay, Mom could perhaps be released.

I was thrilled that her progress was leaps and bounds better. We took many short strolls down the hall with her walker just to make sure. I was pleased that she didn't drag her foot at all. What a relief. The therapists checked her out and finally told us she should stay one more day. Mom resigned herself to that. When Janet came later, she too, was thrilled with the news.

Shortly after Mom's fall, Janet and I had been talking to Aunt Doris, Mom's sister. She had needed a place to stay, so while Mom was in hospital, we said she could have Mom's room at St. Jacobs Place until she returned. Aunt Doris was in reasonably good health so the staff saw that she would be a big help to Mom. The administrator told us that a two-room suite had opened up. They asked us if we might be interested. We all decided it would work out nicely. Aunt Doris would only be charged a minimum rate for meals, and we all agreed that it was a good solution.

We were amazed at how God answered our prayers. Accommodations for her sister Doris. And care for Mom when she was released from the hospital. A win-win situation.

I was happy for Mom, for Aunt Doris, and for myself. I had hoped to join some of my friends at Cobourg Camp for our annual "Girl's Getaway" on Wednesday following Mom's discharge from the hospital. After Mom's fall, I thought I'd have to miss this year, but God made sure everything worked out so I could go after all. My birthday couldn't have been better.

Unexpected Blessings

Sometimes things don't go as planned. I certainly didn't relish the idea of spending my birthday in the hospital with Mom, but it turned out to be delightful. It is easy to judge a situation early but wait and see what God has in store for you. It may just be better than you could have imagined. All caregivers need a break once in a while. God knows that.

Talking to God

God, thank You for nice surprises. Forgive me when I complain ahead of time. Help me to look on the bright side and see what You have in store for me. Because You see the future, You can arrange for special surprises, like the cleaning lady greeting me at the elevator door, to wish me a happy birthday. You alone know what I need, when I need it, and delight in making it happen. You never fail to amaze me. Amen.

Being a Servant

You call Me Teacher and Lord, and you say well, for so I am. If I then, your Lord and Teacher, have washed your feet, you also ought to wash one another's feet.
John 13:13-14

I was honoured to give my mother a sponge bath in the hospital. After, I soaked her feet in the soapy water and then washed them. As I was on my knees before her, scrubbing her feet, I was reminded of how Jesus washed the disciple's feet. It gave me great pleasure to do this for my precious Mama. I helped her clean her dentures, put on a clean nightgown, and then made sure she had her rubber-soled socks on properly. She said she felt like a new woman.

The day before, I had gone to see Aunt Doris at St. Jacobs Place and picked up a few things for Mom, including her Bible and a Hymnal. After Mom was feeling as fresh as a daisy, I picked up the hymnal and we began to sing the beautiful old song: "Be still my soul, the Lord is on your side. Bear patiently, the cross of grief and pain. Leave to thy God to order and provide; In every change, He faithful will remain. Be still, my soul; thy best, thy heavenly Friend. Thro' thorny ways leads to a joyful end."[4]

We were both crying as we sang, but they were good tears and we chuckled at ourselves after.

Good, heartwarming memories.

Janet came to relieve me once I got her caught up on the latest developments with Mom. I must say it was good to get home and put my feet up.

---

[4] By Katharina A. von Schlegel, 1752. Public Domain

Precious Moments

Take time to treasure the small sacrifices you make for the one you care for. It doesn't have to be much, but they will be blessed by your love and tenderness, and in turn, you will have a feeling of satisfaction.

Talking to God

Jesus, when You washed the disciples' feet, some of them were horrified at the thought, but when You did this, You gave me an amazing example of how to serve others. May I never shy away from an opportunity to be a servant. Both servant and server will be blessed. Amen.

Free at Last!

I love the Lord, because He has heard
My voice and my supplications.
Psalm 116:1

I almost had a panic attack when I first went into Mom's room on the morning of her discharge. Her side of the semi-private room was completely empty.

"But I'm supposed to take Mom home today. How can this be happening?"

I scurried down the hall to the nurses' station and asked where my mother was. The nurse told me they moved her last night because the semi-private room where she was originally, was being made into a male room. They thought Mom would feel better in a ward with women. Oh my, what a relief to find Mom safe and sound, sleeping in the other room.

Once the therapists and the doctor at the hospital said that Mom could be discharged, there was a lot of cheering and jumping up and down. Well, now that I think of it, maybe it was just me doing the jumping (with Mom's hip surgery and all) but we rejoiced aloud as we got her dressed. A volunteer came to take Mom down to the lobby in a wheelchair. She waited with her while I got the car from the parking garage one last time. Oh, how good that felt.

My precious Mama was thrilled to be out and about after her ordeal. On our way home, we passed by one of the houses she lived in as a little girl, so it made for a special time as she commented on her happy memories there.

Janet and her husband, Hank, were setting things up at Mom and Aunt Doris's new suite. Mom was happy to be home. I helped her change and got her settled into bed, thankfully leaving Aunt Doris to look after her.

All in all, it was a great day. We were full of thanksgiving that Mom was safe at home in her own bed and more than happy to be among familiar things once again. All was well

Good to be Home

Doesn't it feel good to be home after a hospital stay or even a vacation? There's something about home that makes us happy. As we care for those we love, it's good to remember that old phrase, "There's no place like home!"

Talking to God

Oh Father, I thank you for our home. It does not have to be a palace; it could just be one room or many, but when all things familiar are there, it is a good feeling. Bless my loved one today. Amen.

Stronger Every Day

For the eyes of the Lord are on the righteous,
And His ears are open to their prayers; …
1 Peter 3:12a

Mom was always healthy for most of her life, and a fast healer. Even at age 89, she bounced back quickly after her hip surgery, and we were all amazed and very thankful. In fact, until Mom broke her hip, she was only on one medication for her heart. When she went into the hospital, the nurses asked what meds she was taking. They could hardly believe she took only one. After her surgery she required more medication. That was always a difficult pill for her to swallow (pun intended).

After a few weeks, it became evident that Aunt Doris's help was no longer needed. Besides, they began to get on each other's nerves (as sisters can) and Mom was happy living alone once more.

Problem was, after the anesthetic, the minor dementia symptoms Mom had started to exhibit, worsened. The doctor warned us this could happen. He told us that while not everyone was pushed deeper into their dementia after surgery, many were. We were hoping Mom would be an exception, but soon it became apparent that she was not the exception and thus began her downward spiral.

We knew Mom was often aware of her diminishing faculties, and it frustrated her to no end. We'd try and downplay it, but gradually she believed that if only she were somewhere else, she'd be happy

"I don't belong here," Mom would sometimes say. "You can send me to the *Loony Bin*, but just get me out of here."

We knew that she was in the best possible retirement home. We tried to explain that to her, but her mind simply could not accept it. Often the staff at St. Jacobs Place would call to tell us Mom had threatened to run away. Either Janet or I would have to rush there to calm her down. Often, she'd forgotten she said it, and would be fine, but nonetheless, we'd have to be there, just in case. In a retirement home, there are no locks on the doors, so anyone can run away if they so desire.

Eventually, the head nurse quietly said one day, "If a room opens up over at Heritage House long term care, I think you should take it."

She didn't order us to move Mom, but we knew that her suggestion was wise, and placing Mom in a safer environment would be the best choice. The day soon came that a private room did open up at Heritage House, so we had to make the difficult decision to move Mom over. We knew she maybe wouldn't like it there, but we had little choice. The one good thing was she would be in the same building as Ken. One bright spot, at least.

We desperately wanted to be wrong about Mom not liking it in her new surroundings, but it wasn't to be. Soon, she was demanding we take her back to St. Jacobs Place and was angry at us for moving her. Those were difficult times for Janet and me, but we were powerless to do anything about it.

There were good days of course, where Mom was settled and happy, but gradually those days became less and less, and although we did the best we could, it seemed like it was never enough.

Difficult Times

So often as caregivers, we are frustrated because our hands are tied as to how much we can do for our charges. Sometimes, we have to make difficult choices that can cause the ones we care for to lash out and say things that hurt. But there is nothing else we can do. Guilt wants to take over, but we can't let it. We only have so much control, and even that is sometimes taken from us. To do what we can and leave it sounds easy, but of course it isn't. It's good to ask God to help us in our distress and to give us peace.

Talking with God

God, there are times when I feel like I am at the end of my rope because the one I care for is hurting and I cannot do anything about it. Lord, I desperately need Your help to soothe not only my loved one or those in my care, but also my own heart. Give me Your peace I pray. Amen.

Some Days are Tougher Than Others

My flesh and my heart fail; But God is the strength
of my heart and my portion forever.
Psalm 73:26

Dementia sucks!

I realize that this isn't anything new, but sometimes I get angry and frustrated with this disease and I want to scream at the top of my lungs!

Yesterday afternoon was a glorious time spent with Mom. David and I took her over to her former retirement home to visit her best friend Alice. After we returned, I tucked her into her own bed with a kiss so she could have a nice nap before supper. We left and all seemed right with the world.

Then around 7:00 p.m. I got a phone call from a nurse at Heritage House asking if I would talk to Mom. I knew immediately that something in her mind had switched and she was in turmoil. This time it was because Ken had a bruise on his hand. When I didn't seem too concerned, she told me to send David over because, in her words, "He will know what to do about it. This is serious!"

I carefully explained to Mom that Ken accidently hit his hand on the corner of his dresser, but it wasn't that bad. Mom would not be put off.

"Something must be done about it. Don't you understand how serious this is?" she said.

We went around and around the same mountain, as I calmly told her that I get bruises all the time and they really don't hurt and will heal quickly, but she would not be put off that easily. She was frustrated that I wasn't concerned and felt she needed outside help. Mom moaned again about being in jail where everything is secretive, and no one ever gives her an answer. She then changed tactics.

"Well, I guess all I can do is to go to bed," she said.

"Oh Mom, what a great idea! You get your nice nightgown on and climb into bed and things will look better in the morning."

Of course, that wasn't what she wanted to hear. I think Mom thought for sure I would come running once I realized she wasn't going to do anything about the situation. Poor Mom was frustrated. I could hear it in her voice. I decided to change the subject.

She remembered the lovely visit to St. Jacobs Place that afternoon. "Was I in my right mind then?" Mom asked. When I told her she was, she cried.

"Well, why are things different now?"

"Oh Mom, there's something in your brain that's changed," I said. "You can't help it and I'm sorry."

This didn't seem to help either and she warned me, again, that she was going to get outside help.

The Case of the Bruised Hand. Not sure how our police force would have handled that one. If Mom had her way, she sure would have kept our police force busy. Perhaps we should have called in Sherlock Holmes!

Some days, I figured if I didn't laugh, I would cry. I was sure Mom would not remember all that had happened in the morning. For that, I was grateful. However, *I* remembered, and it took me a while to settle down. Poor David had his hands full between the two of us. Oh dear, oh my!

Life simply does suck sometimes, doesn't it?

At a Low Point

Never feel you are alone in your frustration. It is perfectly acceptable to vent to someone trustworthy, even if there is nothing they can do to help. At least you can share and get it out in the open. Just that act alone can help you deal with difficult situations.

No one is an island and we need each other. We especially need those who understand what we are going through as caregivers.

Talking to God

Oh God. Sometimes I feel so overwhelmed that I cannot think straight. You know my frustrations and the burdens I carry for the one I care for. Give me Your strength and Your grace to get through the bad times, so I can rejoice in the good times. May I never be too proud to admit that I am struggling. Help me to be willing to go alongside others who may also be having a hard time. In this way, we can lift each other up. Amen.

Yellow Jackets Are Nice

You will show me the path of life; In Your presence is fullness of joy; At Your right hand are pleasures forevermore.
Psalm 16:11

Mom loved my yellow jacket. I wore it one day for our breakfast at the Stone Crock Restaurant. Mom had made a huge fuss over my jacket, especially after finding out I bought it at a yard sale for three dollars. Mom and I have always loved bargains.

When David and I stopped in to see her the following day, I wore the same jacket. She went on and on about it again.

"David, you won't lose Nancy as long as she wears that jacket!"

David agreed that it does stand out. "But if she takes it off, I might have trouble identifying her."

Mom thought that was funny and had a good chuckle.

We thought we'd take her to see her friend Alice, but mom was tired and said her bed was calling her name, so I tucked her in, and David and I quietly left her room.

Our next stop was at a local thrift store we frequented often. We shopped for a while and then David was ready to leave. He caught a glimpse of me in another section.

"Excuse me," he said to the three clerks at the till. "Have you seen a lady in a yellow jacket?"

Of course, they spotted me right away and pointed to where I was standing. I saw the whole transaction and thought it was hilarious. We then felt obligated to share Mom's theory that David can't lose me if I wear this jacket. Everyone had a good laugh, including David and me. How much fun can you have with one yellow jacket?

Declutter

Have you ever thought of having a yard sale to get rid of things you no longer wear or use? Maybe sorting through rarely worn clothing and other belongings, could be a good project you could do with the one you care for.

Maybe they would be happy to pass items on that they don't need. It can be a lot of work, but you both could bring someone else a great deal of pleasure, just like the woman who sold me her yellow jacket did. It's also a good way to declutter and to meet your neighbours! You've probably heard the saying, "One man's junk is another man's treasure." Well, it's true! You'd be surprised what one can find at yard sales. Perhaps you should try it out one Saturday. It's fun (trust me, I know).

Talking to God

Lord, You said to give and it shall be given unto me, and sometimes that can mean little things like a yard sale, or even donating articles I no longer need or want, to a local thrift store. Please give me ideas on how to bless others as You have blessed me. Amen.

Fun Phone

... all things are possible to him who believes.
Mark 9:23c

Janet and I decided we should try to find one of those old-fashioned rotary dial phones for Mom; the kind that all you had to do was pick up the receiver to answer and return it to its cradle to hang up. At St. Jacobs Place, she had a handheld, touch-tone phone and often she couldn't figure out how to press 'talk', or how to press 'end'. We also realized it would be a good idea to not leave our phone numbers with her. That way Mom would have to go to the front desk if she wanted to call us. That would help, especially if it was in the middle of the night so the staff could tell her to wait until morning to call.

We liked the idea that one of us could get in touch with her every morning and the other in the afternoon. Janet said she'd make arrangements for a phone to be hooked up as long as David and I could find that kind of a phone.

We figured we would maybe find an older phone at a thrift store, and by gum there on the shelf in one of the stores we visited, was the exact type we needed. And the best part, the price tag was only three dollars. Can't beat that! We went to the till with it and laid it on the counter.

"Could you get the phone for me?" David said to the clerk. She smiled and played along and picked up the receiver.

"Hello? Hello?" Of course, we all had a good laugh.

Try New Places

David and I love thrift stores and yard sales. It isn't so much what we buy, but how much fun we have doing it. Perhaps you would find just the right treasure for the one you care for there. Is there a thrift store near you?

Talking to God

Show me Father what I can do to lighten my load when I'm able to get out of the house. Perhaps it will be at a yard sale or in a thrift store, but either way, may I delight in the things I see and perhaps purchase a bargain (or two). Amen.

Anticipated Phone

... I myself always strive to have a conscience
without offense toward God and men.
Acts 24:16b

When my phone rang this morning, I was delighted to hear my sister Janet's voice.

"This call is coming to you from Heritage House and Mom's own room."

Her phone was all set up and Janet showed Mom how easy it was to answer and hang up. Hopefully she would remember.

I asked Janet how Mom was feeling about the new phone. I figured she'd also be thrilled.

"Mom is at the end of her rope," Janet said, "because she can't take care of Ken any longer."

Janet and I had agreed that when Mom moved out of the seniors' residence, she would need a private room. We knew she would try to take care of Ken if they shared a room, and she could not possibly handle him. The staff at Heritage House agreed that a private room would be the best choice. Mom could visit Ken whenever she wanted, but she could also go back to her own quiet room and have a nap. Mom was put on the waiting list.

It wasn't long before a private room became available, and it worked out great—or so we thought. Most times Mom was content with the arrangement, but then, when her mind drifted into a dementia fog, she got it in her bonnet that she was responsible for Ken and nothing we said would make her think differently.

Here we thought Mom would be happy to have a phone in her own room, but it turned into a total bust. What a letdown. We knew that dementia had taken over, but hopefully she'd be happy sometime later when she saw the phone in her room.

It sure would be nice to talk to Mom daily and let her know that we hadn't forgotten about her. I would try to call her often, but one never knew what state of mind she was in.

The telephone is a marvellous invention.

Give Me Patience … and I Need It Right Now!

There are times when our loved one is struggling and they don't want to heed our ideas, and we feel frustrated. But we must be careful not to allow our disappointment to show. Sometimes a gentle hug and a little prayer is enough.

Talking to God

Oh God, sometimes I am so disappointed that things didn't go the way I'd anticipated. Help me not to dwell on those times. Teach me how to continue to love and accept the present state my loved one is enduring at the moment. Amen.

Mom's Clothes Advice

"… because your heart was tender, and you humbled yourself before the Lord … I also have heard you," says the Lord.
2 Kings 22:19a, c

One of my friends recommended that I try to remember the Mom I knew and loved for all these years past; before dementia hit. Her suggestion made me think of a cute story.

Because Daddy died when I was an immature 14-year-old girl, I was innocent of the ways of men. I had two sisters, so there were only the four girls in our home which included Mom. Because of the lack of men around the house, I continued to be blissfully unaware. Maybe naïve is a better word.

One Sunday morning I came skipping downstairs in my dress for church. Mom took one look at me and I saw horror on her face. I'd forgotten to put my slip on underneath my dress. She told me, in no uncertain terms, that she could see through my skirt. She sent me back to my room with little explanation other than to dress properly.

That brief moment left a deep impression that it must have been ugly to be able to see through a girl's dress. I never forgot that lesson. It wasn't until David and I were married that the subject came up. I told him the story and David laughed.

"Oh Nancy," he said. "It's not ugly at all, but quite sexy!"

It is? Go figure! Maybe Mom didn't know everything after all. I tried to erase Mom's words from my mind, but then it happened.

We were the special guest speakers at a church one Sunday morning, and—you guessed it—I somehow forgot to put on a slip that morning. I didn't discover my faux pas until I was in the ladies' room at the church, right before we were supposed to go up and speak to the large congregation. To my horror, as I looked closely in the mirror, I could see through my skirt. We were scheduled to go on within minutes. I was beside myself. I was about to talk and sing about Jesus to children and adults, wearing a dress that was becoming more and more sheer by the moment. The old 'mom tape,' that it was an ugly sight, filled my mind, along with the revelation from David that it was sexy. I'll never forget the shame I felt during the entire 40-minute program that seemed to go on forever. I couldn't wait until we were finished so I could safely sit down on the front pew.

I didn't have time to confess my horror to David until on the drive home. My wonderfully encouraging husband assured me that in order to see through a skirt, one has to stand with a backlight of some kind, and that church did not have it. I was safe. I breathed a huge sigh of relief and remembered that the ladies' room had a window that would have highlighted that I was not wearing a slip! It never happened again.

Show and tell

Do you have a few stories to tell the one you are caring for? If so, write them down in a special journal so you don't forget them. Then bring them out when the time is right. It may even give you a laugh or two to share an embarrassing moment you've had, and it may well give you both a lift.

Talking to God

Father, I ask that You remind me of the good times I have experienced in the past. Even if it is an embarrassing moment, remind me to share it with others so we can all have a good laugh. Thank You. Amen.

Drive in the Country

The Lord repay your work, and a full reward be given you by
the Lord God of Israel, under whose wings
you have come for refuge.
Ruth 2:12

"What an adventure we had today!"

Those were Mom's words as I tucked her into her comfy bed for a much-needed nap after our time together.

David had found a bike to buy in Waterloo for his bicycle business. Before we went to pick up the bike, we stopped in at Heritage House to ask Mom if she wanted to come along for the ride. She readily agreed. We whisked her away and both of us sat in the backseat while David drove.

He chuckled and said, "I feel like I'm driving Miss Daisy!"

David took a pleasant country route to where the bike was, and then Mom and I sat in the car while he did business with a customer. Mom repeated the same things again and again about being on an adventure, but she was delighted just to sit in the car and look at the scenery.

After David was finished, we took her for a hamburger, fries, and the all-important ice cream treat. She loved every bite.

After our tasty lunch, David offered to take us somewhere shopping, but Mom was fading fast.

"We've been gone such a long time and we did so much!"

I guess to Mom, sitting in a car while David worked, and eating lunch out, seemed like a lot of work to her.

When we were leaving, she said, "You know, I don't even know how to act in a restaurant anymore."

"What could you possibly do wrong, Mom?" I said.

"Well, I could mess my drawers!"

"That is true Mom, that is true."

Go for a drive

Sometimes even a short car ride can lift the spirits of someone who is housebound. It doesn't take much, but a simple trip out of the house or facility could mean a lot to both of you.

Talking to God

God, sometimes I feel locked into routines and see no way out. Give me wisdom to see beyond the four walls and help me create a mini adventure, and sweet memories. Amen.

Accidents Will Happen

A soft answer turns away wrath,
But a harsh word stirs up anger.
Proverbs 15:1

Janet and I had taken Mom to our favourite restaurant for breakfast. There was nothing wrong with Mom's appetite. She ate everything on her plate, like a field hand. It was a delight to see her eat so well, but as we were waiting for our bill Mom said, "I have to go potty." I told her I'd take her.

"No, I'd rather wait until I get to my room."

I didn't argue.

A few minutes later, Mom changed her mind, quickly.

"I don't think I can wait!"

I rushed her, as fast as you can rush a 90-year-old mother, to the bathroom. Just as we got inside, she said, "Uh-oh. Too late!"

I pushed her into a stall and told her to hurry and get on the toilet. It wasn't an easy task and there were a few challenging moments. But we finally did manage to get Mom cleaned up as best we could for the time being. We needed to get her into the car and back to her room—right away. Janet rushed off so she could drive the car close to the door.

Meanwhile, I helped Mom into her pants. I had already rinsed out her underwear in the sink and was clutching them as discreetly as I could, rolled up in wad of paper towels. We tried to stroll through the restaurant in a nonchalant manner, toward the exit sign. On the way out, Mom leaned toward me and with a twinkle in her eye and in a stage-whisper said, "Act as if nothing's wrong."

I couldn't help but roar, and then at the door she said, "If anyone who even looks remotely like me walks into this restaurant, the staff is going to say, "Don't let that woman enter!"

I laughed again.

We finally made it back to her room. Janet rang for the nurses to help. We'd had enough. And wouldn't you know it, just as we got Mom settled down, the fire alarm went off. We couldn't help but laugh as we waited out in the hallway for the all clear.

After taking Mom back to her room, Janet and I told her we had to go home. We kissed her goodbye. But just before we left, she gave us one more reason to giggle.

"Girls. Thank you. Now I feel clean on the outside *and* the inside!"

Janet and I laughed all the way to the car. While everything was happening, it was anything but funny, but our lovely Mom managed to turn it into a comedy routine.

"Nancy, you'll have pages and pages to tell your friends."

You've gotta love a woman who doesn't mind sharing what happened to her, as long as it brings on laughter ... and laugh we did.

Life is What We Make It

We all have stories. Perhaps they are not funny at the time, but sometimes if we look at situations from a different angle, they can become hilarious. If we tell stories about those we care for, though, we need to make sure that doing so doesn't cause embarrassment. If you can't share an embarrassing situation with others, the best idea is to remember it as a funny situation and then have a good laugh yourself. You'll feel better.

Talking to God

Lord, You made me the way I am, and that way can sometimes include me finding myself in the middle of an embarrassing moment or two. However, You also gave me a sense of humour, so help me to look at it from that perspective. It's a great way to relieve anxiety. Amen.

Antidote for Depression

... Be strong and of good courage; do not be afraid,
nor be dismayed, for the Lord your God
is with you wherever you go.
Joshua 1:9b

We found Mom in Ken's room leaning over him while he was in his chair. I couldn't hear what she was saying to him, but I touched her back gently once I realized Ken was sound asleep.

"I keep missing opportunities to help Ken, and I'm feeling so guilty." Mom turned to me with tears in her eyes. I asked what she was missing.

"I keep blowing it when I could make his life better."

She told me she wanted us to wake Ken up so we could take him back to her room. She thought her room was a bit cooler, and Ken would like that.

"Mom, it would be cruel to wake him up. He looks comfortable and if you notice, he isn't sweating."

She didn't seem to grasp what I was saying but did allow me to turn her walker around so we could go back to her room.

"They ignore Ken," Mom said as I walked with her back to her room. "I saw them give strawberry pie to every man but him."

This puzzled me. I knew there had been a baking session in the activity room so when I saw the gals with the finished strawberry pies, I asked them about it.

"Only those who helped make the pie got a piece," the activity director said, "and of course, Ken didn't help make them."

That bit of information didn't help Mom.

She looked so dejected that my heart constricted. Her head was bowed, and her face was drawn. I tried to get her out of her funk and eventually we began to remember all the funny things she had said recently.

Soon we were laughing so hard that one of the workers came into the room to offer refreshments.

"I thought for sure a TV was on," a worker said. I assured her that it was just us, and besides, Mom didn't even have a television. Someone thought we were a comedy sitcom! I think that's a compliment. Life is good right now and I am one thankful daughter.

Feels Good to Laugh

Most everyone feels depressed at one time or another. Some may even think life hardly seems worth living. Caregivers can be particularly prone to feelings of despair; like they are going it alone. This is where it's good to recall, if possible, some of the funny or cute things that have happened, and the mood will most likely change.

Talking to God

Oh God. You see me when life is difficult and there doesn't seem to be any way out. You promised that the joy of the Lord is my strength, so I am asking for joy. You are the giver of good gifts to Your children, and, oh boy—we need joy! Amen.

Lunch with Family

For God so loved the world that He gave His only begotten Son, that whoever believes in Him should not perish but have everlasting life.
John 3:16

I arrived at Mom's room to take her out for lunch, only to find she was in her nightgown ready to climb into bed.

"Oh Nancy, I went for a walk today and I'm ready for a nap," she said.

I told her I'd let her sleep for 20 minutes while I signed the paperwork required to take her out. I was reluctant to wake her up but thankfully she didn't make a fuss. She allowed me to dress her and off we went.

"I'm just being an obedient child," she said over and over, giggling each time.

We met my Aunt Barb and my cousin, Karen, at a cozy restaurant and enjoyed a nice lunch together. At one point, Mom was complaining about her tablemates at Heritage House and how they speak so softly that she can't understand them. Then my aunt, sitting across from her, leaned over to her daughter, Karen.

"What did Flo just say?" my aunt asked.

The four of us laughed at the irony of it all. My cousin Karen showed us a picture of an adorable little boy that her daughter and son-in-law were adopting.

Mom quipped to her sister-in-law, "Barb, we never thought of adoption, did we?"

"Well you didn't have to. You had your own children." Karen said.

Mom didn't skip a beat. "And it was fun!"

Time to listen

Older people especially love to stroll down memory lane every so often. They may not recall what they had for breakfast, but they do remember being young and oh how they love to talk about their adventures. Take time to listen and you will glean much wisdom and history. Also, if you have a video camera, set it on a tripod and hit record, if no one minds.

Talking to God

Father, sometimes I am guilty of rushing through duties and I fail to sit down and really listen. Help me to be reminded to take time out of my busy schedule and then simply ask questions and listen patiently to the answers. I just might be in for a surprise. Amen.

Death in the Family

Those who sow in tears
Shall reap in joy.
Psalm 126:5

I had the very difficult task of telling my Mom that her sister-in-law, and best friend, Barbara, had died. There was a message on our machine from my Aunt Gloria saying my Aunt Barbara had a stroke and had died in the hospital, with Karen by her side. How very thankful we all were that we got together for lunch a few days before and had such a nice time. Little did we know when we said goodbye, we would never see her again on earth.

We knew that Barbara loved God and was ready for Heaven. That gave us peace. Karen told us that her mom had said that next week she would be dancing. Karen wondered if her mother had a premonition. She'd been in a wheelchair for a couple of years and in constant pain, so even though we missed her, we were thankful that she was released from suffering.

Once I told Mom the news, it took a while before it sank in, but then the tears began to flow. She was happy for her sister-in-law because she was free from pain. But Barbara had been a dear friend over the years, too. She was sad that we would no longer be getting together like we had been doing from time to time for our special "breakfast (or lunch) with the moms," as we called it. We talked about how we would miss all the love and laughter. It hurt.

My Aunt Barbara loved flowers so we smiled thinking about how she would be dancing through God's gardens and seeing our loved ones who'd gone on before. What a reunion.

Goodbye Aunt Barbara. You were an inspiration.

Goodbyes Hurt

Life is not only seemingly short, no matter how long we live, it is also unpredictable. One minute our loved ones are with us, and in the next moment they are gone. We truly need to treasure each other every day for we do not know when our last goodbye will actually be our final one.

Talking to God

Jesus, I thank You for making it possible for me to go to Heaven. You took my punishment on the cross in order that I would be declared, "Not guilty." It is a gift that I must receive, but what a gift it is! Thank you for those who are in Your presence even now. What glorious experiences they must be having. Amen.

Reliving Bad News

For God has not given us a spirit of fear, but of power and of love and of a sound mind.
2 Timothy 1:7

My heart ached for my Mama. I called her after breakfast. "Oh Nancy, did Barbara die or is she still alive?" Poor Mom. She had forgotten.

I hated to have to tell her again that Barbara had died. But I did. Mom started crying.

"Well, I woke up this morning and remembered that one of my family members had died but I couldn't remember who, but I kind of thought it was Barbara."

She then asked how she died. We talked for a bit and once it sank in again, Mom was happy that Barbara didn't suffer, and no longer needed a wheelchair.

Aunt Barbara had loved her retirement home and took it upon herself to be the one to welcome each new resident, showed them around, and was a friend from then on. The people and the staff loved my Aunt Barbara and she found great fulfillment in her later years. I cannot imagine how empty the place must feel without her.

Mom asked when we last saw Barbara and I told her the story and the name of the restaurant that we all went to just a few short days before she died.

"Oh, I've never been there," Mom said. I had to smile.

"Well, yes, Mom we were all there on Tuesday, remember?"

I could tell it wasn't registering, but she continued on with questions about how Barbara died and when, again and again. Then, all of a sudden, she switched subjects.

"Is Ken still living?"

I assured her that he was.

"Is he living here?"

I told her that she probably would have seen him at breakfast, and then she vaguely remembered watching him slowly walking back to his room.

I was alarmed at how quickly Mom seemed to be going downhill. My mind visited places and I started to wonder when we would get a call about her dying.

Mom had told us over and over not to mourn for her after she died, because she would be in Heaven with Jesus and all would be well. I must say it was wonderful to have that assurance. Mom, after our serious conversation, offered a warning to me.

"Your generation is the next to go you know. It won't be long before you guys start dropping off like flies."

On that 'happy' note, I said to my tired Mama, "Well, have a good nap, Mom."

I mean, what else could one say to that?

Life Can Be Difficult

It is always hard to have to tell someone that a dear friend or family member has passed away. Deliver the news but then make sure you take time to listen to their pain with kind understanding. No matter the age, it is still heartbreaking when someone dies. We need to ask God to help us find the right words.

Talking to God

God, You alone know the length of my days from birth to death. I thank You that because of Your Son's death and resurrection, I have eternal life with You. Help those who are grieving right now and give them Your peace. Amen.

Appreciative Mother

Praise the Lord! Oh, give thanks to the Lord,
for He is good! For His mercy endures forever.
Psalm 106:1

"Oh, this breakfast is delicious!" Mom must have said that at least 20 times when we ate breakfast at a cute little restaurant with my cousin Karen. It got so funny at one point, that I dryly said to Karen, "It's sad that my mom isn't more appreciative!" Mom laughed too.

"But this *is* a fantastic breakfast, don't you think?"

We did have to agree. It was just so doggone cute the way Mom went on and on about her food that day, although we almost hadn't made it to the restaurant that morning.

I had called Mom the night before to warn her not to go to the dining room because we'd be going out for breakfast.

"I'll be there before 8:00 a.m. Okay, Mom?" I had said. She had agreed, but I also told her to tell the staff who called her to the phone, so that they'd know, too. But when I reached her room—no Mom. I happened to spot the manager and told her how I was supposed to be picking Mom up to take her out for breakfast.

"Yes, I heard that, and we are happy for Flo." I was glad the staff had been aware, but I still couldn't find my mother.

I went down the hall and saw her heading toward me.

"Where were you?" she asked. "I thought you were going to take me out for breakfast. I was beside myself thinking you had forgotten!"

I calmed Mom down and took her back to her room. I helped put on her socks and shoes, and a light jacket, and off we went. She told me she was expecting me around 7:00 a.m. for an 8:30 breakfast meeting.

All was well and we ended up making it to the restaurant without another hitch. And now she had eaten heartily. "I'm thinking I could start to eat the dishes!" Mom said, after she'd cleaned her plate. We all laughed again.

On the way to the car I said, "How do you feel now Mom?"

"Like I was drunk!" More laughter!

When I told Karen she laughed, too.

"How would Aunt Flo know what that was like?"

Mom had never had a drink in her life that I knew of, so it was a stretch. But it sure was funny.

When we were in the car, I said, "What would you like to do now?"

"Just sit in the car and watch the people."

So that's exactly what we did. Mom told us how the simple act of sitting in a car was pure luxury for her, and she was as content as a purring kitten.

After a while, I drove the car over to the river, so we could watch the rushing water and appreciate the different shades of green in the grass and the trees as they stood in stark contrast to the blue sky.

We had a terrific morning, but by 11 o'clock, Mom was ready for a little nap. I took her back to her room, tucked her in and kissed her goodbye, thankful that I had my sweet mother and yet another happy memory.

The morning had worn me out too, so when I got home, I told David to find his own lunch, as I headed to bed for a wee nap. Like mother like daughter. She's a bad influence on me!

Happy Days

Be sure to enjoy and appreciate any good days you have with the one you care for. We never know when it will be the last time, and if we treasure our times together, we won't have any regrets.

Talking to God

Oh God, thank You for all Your wonderful gifts. I have so much to praise You for. May I never take the good days for granted but place them in a special memory bank to withdraw the images whenever I need to. Lord, I pray that You give my loved one Your peace and sweet rest. Amen.

Day Out and About

I know that You can do everything, And that no purpose of Yours can be withheld from You.
Job 42:2

My sister, Janet, told me she picked Mom up around 10:00 a.m. to get her out for a while. Janet and her husband, Hank, had a few errands to run. Mom was content to sit and wait in the car. Sure enough, Janet took Mom into Tim Hortons for a coffee and a donut while Hank was doing a few things.

"I feel like a kid in a candy store," Mom said, happily munching on her sticky treat.

Later, Hank picked them up and drove them back to their house for lunch. They sat on the deck, overlooking a farmer's field. Mom loved watching the horses as she happily ate a hearty lunch including a summer sausage sandwich, homemade potato salad, fresh strawberries, and tea. It didn't take much to delight Mom.

After lunch they sat in the living room so Janet could do some work on her computer.

"Anytime you want to take me home, it's okay with me." Mom apparently kept telling Janet.

"Fine," Janet would say and kept working. Mom repeated it a few more times until Janet got the hint. It was refreshing to hear that Mom actually wanted to go home rather than complain. Music to Janet's ears.

"Heritage House is the *best* place for old people!" Mom blurted out as Janet walked her back to her room. When Janet relayed this to me later, we were both surprised that she said that. That was a far cry from the days she wailed, "This is no place for old people!"

"That's great, Mom!" Janet had said that day.

We were all glad that she had finally accepted her new home and we were both glad to hear Mom's glowing words.

Coffee and a Donut can do Wonders

Take a drive in the country or find some food that the one you are caring for remembers and serve it. The food isn't as important as the thought you put behind it. Then, seeing the look on a contented face, when memories of good times come flooding back, makes it worth the effort.

Talking to God

Give me wisdom, Lord, so I can understand a little of the heart of the one I care for. May You give me creativity beyond my capability, for You alone know my heart. Amen.

Digging in a Snowbank

Delight yourself also in the Lord,
And He shall give you the desires of your heart.
Psalm 37:4

"Oh, Nancy!"

It wasn't a good thing to hear first thing during my regular 7:30 a.m. call to Mom.

When she starts off like that, she's usually in a dementia fog and is most likely being unreasonable. But on that particular morning, what she had to say made me howl with laughter. And it sure felt good.

"Oh, Nancy! I had the weirdest dream all night and it wouldn't quit. I dreamed I was trying to dig myself out of a snowbank. I was digging and plowing and working very hard to get out of that snowbank and it never ended. Oh my, but I worked hard!"

Of course, I had to laugh because she was laughing, too.

"It wasn't funny all night, I'll tell you!"

Mom continued. Except the dream changed from snow to pushy friends.

"One of my neighbour ladies came into my room and climbed into bed with me. She kept hogging the bed and soon I fell on the floor and had to sleep on my small couch."

At first, I wondered if it really happened. But Mom assured me that it was still in her dream. She continued to tell me that one of the workers came and took the woman back to her room.

"At first this woman was sitting on my toilet and I thought she had a lot of nerve being in *my* bathroom!"

We both had a good chuckle and it felt good, especially since Mom had calmed down. What a great way to start the day! It didn't always turn out this pleasant, but that day was a bonus that I could put into my "laughter memory bank". Love it, love it, love it.

Have an Interesting Conversation

I may have braced myself for a negative phone call, but it turned out to be a delightful conversation. We just never know how things will turn out and it taught me that I needed to be careful not to pre-judge how a conversation will go. Sometimes it only takes a little spark to turn the mood around and have you both laughing, giggling, or in a much better mood.

Talking to God

God, only You know my heart. Sometimes I can't find anything happy or light about a situation, but You can change the atmosphere if I ask. May I never forget that You are with me always. Amen.

Life Can Be Tough

'Assuredly, I say to you, inasmuch as you did it to
one of the least of these My brethren, you did it to Me.'
Matthew 25:40b

Mom loved it when Janet and I would take her out for breakfast. We tried to make it once a week and it always delighted her. One time after we had eaten a good breakfast, Mom had trouble getting up from the table.

"I'll bet the whole restaurant is laughing at me."

I felt sorry for her.

"Oh mom, no one would ever laugh at an elderly person. In fact, they're probably saying, 'Look at how kind and loving her daughters are.'"

That was good for a laugh. Once we managed to get Mom outside, she wanted to sit on a bench.

We weren't in a rush, so we obliged. After a while we got up and the three of us strolled down main street, arm in arm, until we reached another bench. We sat down again. Mom enjoyed doing that.

Eventually we got Mom in the car and took her back to her cozy room. I helped her onto the bed. Mom's head barely hit the pillow before she was out like a light, and my heart was full of love for this sleeping beauty.

Just before Mom had climbed into bed, she said, "Oh how I wish I would just fall asleep and wake up in Heaven."

I agreed with her that that would be a wonderful way to go, but we both talked about how it isn't up to us. Just before she nodded off, we talked about how God has a perfect plan for her life, and how He alone knows the exact time when He will call her home.

Gifts from Heaven

Walking down main street in a little town can be rewarding and very satisfying, and it doesn't even have to be a long walk.

Just manageable. Being out together, enjoying the sights, and people-watching can be a real highlight for those who spend most of their waking hours indoors. Take a few minutes. Take a stroll with your loved one and find out how rewarding it can be.

Talking to God

I thank you Father that you said that when I help others, I am helping You. I am Your hands and feet here on earth and I want to please You in every way. Give me courage to carry on as I continue to do Your will. Bless those around me and may I be a blessing as well. Amen.

Not the Way We'd Planned

For even the Son of Man did not come to be served, but to serve, and to give His life a ransom for many.
Mark 10:45

Some days just didn't turn out the way we had planned. David and I were looking forward to Sunday lunch with Mom. We were going to splurge on calories and pick up some Kentucky Fried Chicken (KFC). A treat. We hadn't had KFC for years and just knew Mom would be thrilled to have a taste again. Turns out, we were wrong!

I called Mom first thing in the morning to remind her not to go down to the dining room for lunch. I reminded her we would be bringing KFC after church. She was thrilled.

"I think I'll have a nap this morning so I'm ready for you to come," she said.

I called the front desk at Heritage House to tell a staff member because sometimes Mom would forget (who's kidding who. She forgot all the time.)

We arrived with our bag of yummy smelling chicken and went into Mom's room. Our plan was to take her down to the sunroom to feast on our lunch, but Mom was curled up in bed. I called her name, then shook her but she didn't move. I went into panic mode for a few seconds, but then she moaned and opened one eye. She looked up at me. I was relieved.

"Hey Mom, get up, we've got food for you."

She was angry.

"I've had it. I'm at the end of my rope. I can't do this any longer!" she wailed.

I asked her what was wrong, but she just kept repeating the same thing, "Come on, get up," I said again.

"No!"

She was grumpy. There was no doubt.

"Well okay, Mom. Then David and I will just leave and take the food and go home!"

This took her by surprise.

"What do you want me to do?"

I told her that I'd help her get dressed and we'd go down to the sunroom to eat our chicken. She reluctantly agreed and we walked down and put the food out for her. She continued to grumble picking at her food while we ate ours. I must say that my long awaited "treat" turned to sawdust in my mouth.

"I'm just a witch," Mom said over and over, her tone softening. When I told her she wasn't a witch, Mom responded with an expletive that took me by surprise. I burst out laughing.

"Mom, you have such a potty-mouth."

Mom laughed, too.

Finally, David brought a tray of tea and cookies to us. Mom seemed a bit better, but we never did figure out what happened to set her off.

I wondered how and why her mood could have changed so much since I first talked to her at nine o'clock that morning. Like I said, some days just don't go the way they are planned. This day was one of them. Sigh, sigh, and sigh again ... and sigh once more for good measure.

Don't Worry Be Happy

Sometimes we try and try and it just isn't good enough. It can be disheartening. Thing is, the ones we care for often cannot help how they respond. With dementia, the brain malfunctions and no one can do anything about it. You don't need to take the blame when things go wrong. Better to leave it and move on. Next time, perhaps things will be better.

Talking to God

God, sometimes my best efforts fall flat. You see me struggling, Father, and I need Your encouragement. Remind me that You truly understand. May I look to You for patience and ideas of how to reach my loved one. You never leave me or forsake me, even in the darkest hours. I love You. Amen.

Meltdown

… He who has begun a good work in you will
complete it until the day of Jesus Christ;
Philippians 1:6b

What a morning! I was glad to be able to stay home all day and was planning to get some chores done. Then Heritage House called.

"Your mom is having a meltdown," the nurse said, "and she asked me to call you."

The nurse put Mom on the phone, and I asked her what was wrong. She sobbed, saying that she was having a stroke, and no one cared. She told me I had to come at once. I told her I would be there.

I got dressed and called Janet to meet me there. When we arrived, we saw Mom calmly eating her breakfast in the dining room. We didn't interrupt her and went to her room to wait. When a nurse brought her back, Mom started to cry when she saw us. We did what we could to calm her down.

"Well I do remember that someone gave me some advice this morning," Mom said after she was feeling a little better.

"What was the advice?" Janet asked.

Mom gave her a funny look. "Well what *was* the advice?"

Janet and I laughed and said, "How do we know?" Mom didn't get it at first, but soon she joined in the laughter.

Mom had a bit of a lucid moment and asked us what she did this morning to get us to come. We gently told her. Poor Mom was full of remorse and kept apologizing. We kept assuring her that we know she can't help it when her mind does the flip. We assured her that we loved her.

"When I act like that, you should hit me over the head with my pity pot," Mom said.

"We can't Mom. It's full!"

We all laughed again.

Later on, the hairdresser took Mom to the salon to give her a haircut. When she strolled back into the room Mom was obviously in a better mood.

"Well, now I'm all ready for my burial because I've had a bath and now a haircut!"

"All you need now is a shave!" I said. We all had a good laugh once more.

The day may have started off badly, but it ended well. For that we were most thankful.

Let the Chips Fall Where They May

Sometimes we have to rearrange our schedule to meet needs. We can either do it with a happy heart, or with resentment. Our response to situations often dictates the outcome, and even if things don't turn out well, at least we haven't done damage to our own bodies by exhibiting anger, frustration, and worry. Stuff happens. It's better to roll with the punches than fight against them.

Talking to God

Father, I am so thankful that nothing comes as a surprise to You. When I have my days all neatly planned out, You alone know what will transpire and are with me every step of the way. Help me to respond properly and lovingly when it seems as if I simply do not want my routine disrupted. Remind me that You have it all under control. Amen.

Crisis

Be anxious for nothing, but in everything
by prayer and supplication, with thanksgiving,
let your requests be made known to God;
Philippians 4:6

My regular morning phone call to Mom didn't turn out the way I had hoped. Mom answered on the second ring and I could tell she was still in bed.

"Oh Nancy, it's so good to hear your voice. You have no idea how happy this makes me feel."

Then she asked what was new. I started to tell her about how David and I were getting ready to help with our monthly seniors' luncheon. I explained that we would be working in the kitchen. Before I got to the end of my story, I heard a noise. It sounded like someone was dialing.

"Mom, are you there?" I repeated over and over as the dialing sound persisted. No response. I hung up and called again and again. Busy signal every time. I finally gave up knowing that Mom would be on her way to breakfast.

Shortly after 9:00, a nurse from Heritage House called to say Mom was upset because of the discontinued call this morning. She put Mom on the phone. My poor Mama was crying pitifully saying she didn't know what had happened, and she felt no one loved her and we'd decided never to see her again. Of course, I assured her of our love and then told her we'd visit on our way to the senior's luncheon.

We stopped on our way, as promised. I'd packed up some watermelon and some peanut butter fudge for her, but when we arrived, she was sleeping. I'd also brought along a bag containing her fall and winter clothes that I'd stored in our attic. I made some noise putting it all away and she woke up.

"Oh Nancy, I'm so glad to see you." Her face lit up when she saw me. "I was so upset because the phone fell, and I didn't know how to fix it. I was sure you didn't love me anymore."

I assured her again that I did love her and stuff like this happened when her brain went loopy. She laughed. Then she feasted on the watermelon and the fudge which she gobbled down with great delight. We sat and talked for quite a while. Then Mom noticed David's shoes.

"David, what kind of shoes are you wearing?"

"Running shoes."

"Well it looks like they are falling apart!"

We laughed, for even though David had some nice shoes at home, he loved his holey, comfy ones and he didn't apologize for them either!

We chuckled because right after she noticed his dilapidated shoes, she said she was having trouble with her eyesight.

"How can you say your eyes are bad when you noticed David's shoes are falling apart?"

Problem solved—eyes seemed fine.

Soon we had to leave. Mom was ready to climb back into bed anyway, so all was well ... at least for now!

Let Go and Let God

You may find that it doesn't take too much to get someone out of a slump. Other times, it is impossible, but at least you tried. You will never know what sets someone off, but the important thing is that patience and love are the key. The one you care for will benefit and so will you.

Talking to God

Lord, I come to you with empty hands sometimes. I need your strength and wisdom to carry me through. Thank You that You are my strength and that I need not be anxious about anything, but trust that You are in full control. I praise You for Who You are. Amen.

Life Happens

… but God is faithful, who will not allow you to be tempted beyond what you are able, but with the temptation will also make the way of escape, that you may be able to bear it.
1 Corinthians 10:13b

"Oh Nancy, I can't stay here one more day! I'm going to go crazy and you have to get me out of here!" Mom's first words to me when I found her in the dining room were not exactly welcoming. I felt like saying, "Hello Mom, nice to see you too!" but I refrained.

Not too sure what happened to get her so worked up, but one of the Personal Support Workers just smiled at me knowingly. I nodded, smiled back, and gave her the *I'll take over* look.

"Mom, we have an ice cream treat for you in your room. You know how you love that."

She suddenly became happy and gladly followed me down the hall. David came toward us with the promised treat, and we headed outside to sit in the shade.

"Oh my, but this is good." Mom made a huge fuss over her delicious confection. "You know, this has always been my favourite."

"That's why we keep bringing it—because we enjoy seeing you enjoying it!"

Her attitude changed completely, and we were able to go down memory lane to some of the good and funny things that have happened to us over the years. We laughed and laughed.

One incident that put a smile on our faces took place in the mid 1960's. We were all dressed up for a wedding with our fancy hats, gloves, high heeled shoes, and full skirts. After the ceremony, Daddy realized that our car wouldn't start. With many people looking on, Mom steered our old clunker of a car while the others had to push to get it started. Rather than being embarrassed, we howled at the spectacle it must have been.

"I remember that so clearly. We honestly didn't care how it looked, we just wanted to get it started so we could get to the reception!" Mom said.

"Mom, do you recall when we had that clunker with the finicky windshield wipers?"

"Oh yes, I certainly do," she said.

"During sunshine filled days, they would make a "bloop-bloop" sound out of the blue, which made us roar with laughter." But the wipers didn't always want to budge during a rainstorm. If they did work, sometimes one of the blades would fly off, remember?"

Mom smiled, knowingly.

"And we'd have to stop the car and go down into the ditch to retrieve it, all the time laughing hysterically as we got soaked."

"So many memories," Mom said. "It seemed we could laugh at just about anything and it felt good."

When Daddy was alive, he kept all our cars in good condition, but after he was gone, we had to put up with endless problems. Besides that, we could only afford older cars, but Mom took it in stride. She showed us how to accept whatever came, with grace and laughter

After our treat, and much laughter, we took Mom to Ken's room so they could have a visit. When we left, she thanked us for coming.

"Even if I don't remember that you were here, I had a good time," Mom said as we said our goodbyes.

Isn't that sweet?

Forgive and You Shall Be Forgiven

No matter how we were raised, or what our experiences are, there are always things in our lives that we wish we could change. However, that isn't possible is it? We all have choices. We can either moan and groan or complain about the bad things that happened, or we can forgive and carry on. Whenever we hold unforgiveness and bitterness, it poisons us. Forgiveness does not excuse the person who hurt us, but it does set us free.

Talking to God

Father God, I am thankful that You alone know my past, present, and future. You saw me being formed in my mother's womb and You saw what conditions I was raised in and how it affected me, even if I didn't know. I am thankful that You are the restorer and when I put my life in Your hands, You will make beauty from ashes. Nothing is too difficult for You and may I always be aware of that truth. Amen.

Dementia Does Strange Things

… For everyone to whom much is given, from him much will be required; …
Luke 12:48b

My sister, Janet, is home! Hank and Janet had been visiting their daughter and her family in Newfoundland for two weeks and, apparently, had a terrific time. Mom was also pleased that Janet was back. The three of us happily made our way out one morning for breakfast as was our usual custom on a Wednesday.

We ordered our standard fare and, while Mom concentrated on her food, Janet told story after story of all their adventures. Mom finished her breakfast and then looked at our plates.

"How can you girls do all this talking and still eat your food?" she said, pointing at our empty plates.

We told her we are talented that way, but she didn't seem to grasp the concept. We paid our bill, headed back to Heritage house, and helped Mom to her room. We visited some more, but then got talking about how some of her clothes were disappearing. For instance, we hadn't seen her two nightgowns in a while, so we talked to the laundry supervisor who was just as puzzled about it as we were.

In June last year, when Mom was in the hospital, I had brought along a baby pillow for my back.

"Hey Mom, remember that blue baby pillow that I gave you in the hospital when you broke your hip?"

Turned out Mom liked my little pillow so much that she had claimed it. I was glad that she used it all the time but hadn't noticed it around for a while.

"Do you know where it is, Mom?"

"I don't know," she said, when I asked her about it.

I ended up finding a similar one at the thrift store on our next visit. I bought it and she was most pleased.

When Janet saw the new baby pillow and heard my story about how the other one disappeared, she remembered something.

"You know, one day I was visiting Mom and saw a bunch of stuffing in her waste basket. When I asked about it, she had no clue as to how it got there, and I just forgot about it. Now that I think of it, it did look like the stuffing from a pillow."

We surmised that when Mom was experiencing one of her dementia episodes, she must have ripped it apart and thrown it away. One never knows what Mom will do during these spells.

It was good to have Janet back. I sure did appreciate her support. We left Mom in her room to have a nap while we went together to the department store to pick up two nightgowns to replace the missing ones. We made sure that the laundry department received them and would iron on Mom's name. After she woke up from her nap, we showed Mom the new nighties.

"Oh girls. I love these nightgowns. They are so soft and pretty," Mom said, stroking them gently. "I just hope these don't get up and walk away."

Janet and I looked at each other and smiled.

"Yes Mom, we too hope they don't walk away."

Lost and Found

Sometimes, you just have to "go with the flow." We always laugh at that statement because Mom's name was "Flo." And sometimes we just have to go along with her as well!

When we, as caregivers, see things that are wrong, we can either make a fuss or just let some things slide, as long as there is no danger. It's far easier to let things go than to carry them around. Problems can easily accumulate and can become a heavy load. It's best to release them so we'll feel much better.

Talking to God

God, I thank you so much that You never give up on me. I fail you time and time again, but you will always forgive me if

I ask. My slate is wiped clean once again. Help me to do the same for those around me. It is so easy to hold a grudge against someone, but that is not Your plan. You say, "Forgive as you have been forgiven" and I've been forgiven a great deal. May I simply carry on with the clean heart You give me so I can be everything I was created to be. Amen.

More Than One Birthday

A man who has friends must himself be friendly,
But there is a friend who sticks closer than a brother.
Proverbs 18:24

Sunday morning, I called the front desk at the home and told the receptionist that David and I would be bringing lunch in for Mom. I asked if someone would make sure she would stay in her room. The receptionist said she'd let the staff caring for her know.

We ended up having a fire drill at church, so that made the service a bit longer. We then had to pick up hamburgers for lunch, so we were even later getting to Heritage House. My heart sank when Mom wasn't in her room. I ran down to the dining room, but she wasn't there.

"Flo is in the sunroom waiting for you," one of the workers said. I was relieved. We walked in with our bag of food.

"Oh, I thought you'd forgotten me," Mom said. "I was sitting on my pity pot feeling very sorry for myself, especially since it's my birthday."

I apologized and told her about the fire drill.

"Mom, your birthday isn't until September 25th and it's only September 2nd."

Her brow furrowed.

"Mom, you haven't even touched your hamburger. Don't you want to taste it?" Mom didn't say anything, but obviously the fries were tasty, and it appeared as if she hated to move from them.

Finally, she bit into her hamburger a few times, but then spotted the chocolate milkshake. She took a slurp and ignored the rest of her hamburger and fries. No coaxing could get her to budge from her shake. She didn't stop until she was at the very bottom of the cup and by that time, was no longer interested in the hamburger or fries.

"I still need something else," she said, still turning her nose up at the hamburger.

"How about some coffee and cookies? Would you like that, Mom?" I said.

Her face brightened up.

"Oh, coffee and cookies would be wonderful," she happily noted.

David went down to the kitchen and brought back a pink tray loaded with two cups of coffee and a glass of juice for himself, along with a small plate of assorted cookies.

"What a great birthday party this has been." Mom beamed.

I mentioned again that it wasn't her birthday, but she didn't catch on, so we dropped it. I guess all I can say is, "Happy Birthday dear Mama, Happy Birthday to you!"

Time to Celebrate

Every day can be a celebration. We don't have to wait for a certain date to celebrate a birthday, anniversary, or Christmas. It's okay to take advantage of today. Think of ways to do something special that will brighten up everyone involved, especially the one for whom you care.

Talking to God

I thank You Father that every day can be a cause to celebrate Your goodness, love, and mercy. I realize that whatever good I have, comes from Your hand and I am aware that I have much to be thankful for. Bless the one I care for and help me to help them see all the good things in life. May we both truly enjoy your blessings. Amen.

Laughter

A merry heart makes a cheerful countenance, …
Proverbs 15:13a

After visiting Mom one day, Janet and I spoke with one of the Personal Support Workers. She asked us if it was acceptable for a staff member to call one of us if Mom had a meltdown. We assured her that would be perfectly fine. Janet or I were usually able to talk Mom down when she was upset. Not to mention, we were glad to be there for our mother, even if it meant just talking to her on the phone.

"Your family has such a good sense of humour, and that helps greatly," one of the workers said.

Our family had always laughed easily and understood how laughter lightened most situations and took away tension. The Bible says, "A merry heart does good, like medicine,"[5] and it's true. We were glad that we laughed so easily. I think it was a gift that we unwrapped often.

When Janet or I got one of those frantic calls, Mom usually started off her tirade with how bad it was, and that we had to come immediately. We learned the pattern. But after a while she calmed down. Sometimes all we needed to do was remind her of something good that happened, or something funny from our past. When we did that, she'd soon forget what upset her. Sometimes we suggested she ask for a nice cup of tea or a hot chocolate. Usually she decided that was a good idea and we would hang up on a happy note.

We'd often watched the staff in action when they did not see us, so we knew that they were very loving and tender, and that Mom was in good hands. This was most important to our family and we'd often mentioned our gratitude to them and apologized for Mom's outbursts. They'd laugh it off indicating

---

[5] Proverbs 17:22 NKJV

that it was part of their job. They thanked us for our compliments and carried on to the next crisis. We were deeply impressed with all their hard work and the patience these workers had. God bless them!

Encouragement Goes a Long Way

If the one you love is in long-term-care, try to give the workers a thumbs up from time to time. Often the workers have unpleasant jobs, but most seem to do it with great care and gentleness. We must also keep in mind that they are only human and may have bad days, too. I've found that bringing in a treat for the staff once in a while, also helps lift their mood. If you are the 24/7 caregiver, find ways to refresh yourself, otherwise you will wear down and then you will be no good to anybody. Don't be afraid to ask for help. You need time for yourself, too.

Talking to God

I thank You God for the workers that care for the one I love day and night. They are on the front lines and often their jobs are mighty difficult. Guide me in ways I can encourage them and show them how much I appreciate their dedication. Thank You for each one of these precious men and women. For those who are full time caregivers, may You show them how to get much-needed breaks and, most importantly, to disregard any guilty thoughts about being selfish. Even Jesus slipped away from time to time to be by Himself. By His example, I should realize how important it is. Amen.

Growing Old Isn't for Sissies

And we know that all things work together for good to those who love God, to those who are the called according to His purpose.
Romans 8:28

When I called Mom on the phone today, she sounded a bit uptight.

"Oh Nancy, I'm so glad you called," she said. "You know, they had a fire drill here, but I wasn't dressed, so I waited for someone to come into my room, but no one did. If this would have been a real fire, I'd have burned." (Now how should I have responded to that?)

The more I talked to her, the more I figured out that she must have heard a noise when she was napping and thought it was a fire drill. Turned out there was no drill, although it was very real to Mom. I assured her that the staff were well-trained and would look in every room, do a head count and make sure everyone is accounted for. I told her that if that didn't happen, then there was no fire drill. She had trouble understanding, so I decided to change the topic.

"Do you remember that David and I were here yesterday?" I asked.

"You were? What did we do?"

"David and I brought you an ice-cream treat, and then we sat outside while you ate it."

"I did?"

"Yes, and then we visited Ken a bit later. I gave you some homemade peanut butter fudge to share with him."

"You did?"

"Yup. And, on Saturday, Hank and Janet were here visiting and you sat outside with them too."

"I did?"

"Yup."

I told her the time and reminded her that it would soon be time for supper.

"It is?"

"Yup. Are you dressed?"

"No, I'm not. What do I do?"

It was heartbreaking to realize that my mother didn't even remember how to dress herself. When we were children, she made sure that our clothes were clean, mended, and tidy, and now she is having difficulty taking care of herself. It was like our roles had reversed.

"Okay, Mom. Put on a blouse and a pair of slacks and then either a pair of slippers or shoes. Can you do that Mom?"

"Well, I have a striped top on, and a pair of blue slacks partially on, is that OK?"

"Oh yes Mom, that's perfect!" I was happy to hear she was dressed already.

"All you need to do is pull up your slacks and put something on your feet and you're good to go!"

"But I need to put on a top."

"Didn't you just say you had a top on?"

"Oh yes, a striped top."

"Good, Mom. That will be fine. I am sure you look lovely. So, all you have to do next is pull up your slacks and put on your slippers or shoes."

"And then I can go down to the dining room?"

"Yup."

"Well, I guess I can do that. Can you come and help me?"

"No. Sorry, Mom. I have to make supper. But you'll be fine."

We went through the drill another two times. Finally, she got it.

"Well, Nancy. Okay. Bye."

Growing old definitely isn't for sissies.

Some Days Are Better Than Others

Patience is a word we need to remember every day. Some days are full of more questions than answers, and even when you do give an answer it sometimes doesn't compute to those dealing with dementia. It's like a fog. Nothing can penetrate.

It's important to realize that he or she does not want to be this way anymore than we want them to be. It must be terrifying not to know what to do next. This is when patience is most needed, and, sometimes, the most difficult to give. Hang in there!

Talking to God

Oh Lord, I need patience. There are so many times when I'd like to shake some sense into the one in my care, but I must be reminded that they don't mean to lack judgement. I ask for Your divine intervention to give me the needed love and understanding to get through the day. Thank You for loving me and for having great patience with my own faults and failures, so that I can pass on that love and patience to others. Amen.

Low Self-Esteem

Peace I leave with you, My peace I give to you; not as the world gives do I give to you. Let not your heart be troubled, neither let it be afraid.
John 14:27

When Mom heard my voice that morning, she was once again ready with her list.

"Oh Nancy, I'm so glad you called because I have a lot I need to ask you."

"Sure Mama. Fire away!"

There was a pause. I could sense she was racking her brain for something to tell me and it wasn't there. I couldn't imagine how that must have felt. My heart ached for her.

"Well, a woman keeps coming into my room and looking at my blue housecoat and I'm afraid she might take it sometime," she finally said.

I assured Mom that even if that woman did take it, the staff would know it belongs to her and they would return it to her closet. This helped calm her down a bit.

"Flo, it's time for supper!" I heard someone shout to Mom.

"Oh, I guess I'd better get dressed because it's time for supper." Mom sounded a bit better.

"You mean you don't have any clothes on?"

"I don't have any coleslaw?" I laughed so hard on the other end of the phone that Mom finally asked me what she said.

She had a good laugh too when I told her.

"So, Mom, go put some coleslaw on and go to supper already!"

No One Has It All Together

Those with dementia or Alzheimer's can imagine all kinds of things and often become paranoid because they don't understand what is happening. It is important that we don't get angry at them for feeling this way, for it is very real for them.

Hopefully you can soothe the poor person's soul, but if not, try to change the subject or think of something funny to laugh at. You'll both feel better.

Talking to God

It is so easy to fluff off the one in my care and think that they are either eccentric or plain wrong in their thinking., But this is often a harsh way to look at things. Remind me, Lord, that I have never walked in their shoes, but You were there with them every step of their lives. You alone understand their thinking. Give me wisdom to know how to handle each unique situation with love and understanding. Amen.

Good Things in Our Mouths

Bless the Lord, O my soul; And all that is within me, bless His holy name! Who satisfies your mouth with good things, So that your youth is renewed like the eagle's.
Psalm 103:1,5

"I have a feeling today will be strange."

These were the words Mom greeted me with when I walked into her room at 8:30 a.m. with food. I was hoping she was wrong.

Janet and I had decided to take breakfast to Mom rather than take her out on this particular morning, so I picked food up at a fast food restaurant on the way in and it worked well.

After we finished putting our food on the table in the sunroom, I began saying the blessing, but Mom was totally in her own world. She hadn't heard me praying and started talking. I quickly said, "Amen" and Janet and I dug in.

Mom looked at us, at her food, and quietly bowed her head and prayed and then whispered, "Thank You Jesus" twice. Her words gave us pause that she was so close to God.

Mom thoroughly enjoyed her egg muffin and coffee.

"I've never had this before and it's good!"

Janet and I both smiled. We both knew she had often enjoyed this kind of breakfast before but, hey, we didn't think she needed to be reminded of that. And when Mom was happy, we were happy.

A bit later, Janet remembered the chocolate she'd brought the day before. She opened it up and we dug in. We all agreed it was delicious.

"I've put so many good things into my mouth today!" Mom said, looking satisfied.

I loved that phrase and thought perhaps we should make this statement a habit after every good meal. But the gladness was not to last. Back in her room, Mom began to cry.

"Was I good to Jane?" she wanted to know. We assured her that she was indeed a good mother to Jane, our sister who had died, and then she tearfully asked if she was good to us. Again, we assured her that she had been a wonderful mother and she still was.

"Did I have a good life?"

Both Janet and I enthusiastically replied that she had a very good life. She cried some more.

"What did I do to deserve that?"

I said, "Mom, you were always very faithful to God and His Word. You freely gave to others and He poured out His blessing on you."

Mom was listening.

"In fact, He blessed you with us!" Mom brightened up as I gestured to Janet and me.

"Oh yes, He certainly did!" Mom was laughing by now, although she seemed quite confused.

"Well, you know that I am here to guide you, right?" she said, tongue in cheek.

We had to laugh and totally agreed that we knew this bit of information to be true.

Janet and I had no idea what Mom's premonition about "it being a strange day" would bring. In actuality, it turned to be quite delightful for us all. It was different, so that could be what she was anticipating.

Because taking breakfast to Mom in her room was a success and less stressful for Janet and me, we decided we would do it again.

And in Mom's words: "Put more good things into our mouths."

Enjoy Good Food

So often we take things for granted. How many times have you put food in your mouth without appreciating the taste and the unique texture? We often take a bite, chew, swallow, and continue on until it is finished without really tasting it. God gave us flavorful food to enjoy and to give us health and strength to carry the load of being a caregiver. It is important that we take care of ourselves. Take time to savour your food and thank God for the ability to taste and don't feel guilty for taking that time for yourself. It will surprise you with pleasure!

Talking to God

Oh God, please help me to enjoy the bounty of food you have given me. You know that I need Your strength to continue caring for the one You have entrusted me with. May I make the right choices and savour every bite. Help me to give thanks for all You've given to me, so I in turn, can help others. Amen.

A Taste of Home

A father of the fatherless, a defender of widows,
Is God in His holy habitation.
Psalm 68:5

Pizza. That's what David and I had decided to take to Mom for lunch after church. I'd called the staff to tell them we were coming with food, so we picked up the pizza right after the service. To my dismay, Mom wasn't in her room when we arrived. I finally found her sitting outside the dining room looking dejected.

"See Flo. I told you your daughter would come!" the nurse said when she saw me. Mom looked up but I could tell she was struggling.

"Come on Mom," I said, trying to sound cheerful. "We're going to the sunroom to have pizza."

She followed me.

"Do you know that Ken and I are falling apart?" Mom kept asking the question over and over until we arrived at the sunroom.

"Mom, you and Ken do have some difficulties, but you are in a great place where they know how to take good care of you both. Besides, we have pizza waiting for us in the sunroom down the hall," I said.

Mom's eyes got really big when she saw the pizza box and the soda pop. She made a huge fuss about how depressed she was before, but how happy she was now because of the pizza feast. Every bite and every sip were met with great appreciation and delight. David and I grinned.

"I felt so out of the loop all morning," Mom said every so often in between bites of pizza.

"But God knew we were coming and was whispering, 'Just wait and see what I have planned for you at noon!'"

She brightened up when I said that, and we continued eating.

When I pulled out a package of chocolate macaroons, Mom ate one right after the other. Both the pizza and macaroons were a taste from the past and it made her day.

It turned out to be a great time with Mom. How thankful I was that God put it on our hearts to take pizza and chocolate macaroons to her. After all, God does know best, and He knew His precious daughter Flo needed a lift (and some chocolate) And we received benefits from it too.

God's Plan Is Best

Only God is omnipresent and can listen to billions of prayers all at the same moment. This means, when He softly directs us to do something for someone else, no matter how odd it may seem, we need to obey. He knows exactly what will do the most good. Practice the habit of quietly listening for God's still small voice that will guide you to paths you never thought of, and it will be fabulous!

Talking to God

Father, You promised that You would guide me with Your eyes. This means I must sit at Your feet and look into Your face, which takes time and a conscious decision to do so. May I never try to do things on my own but rely heavily on You for direction. Thank You that Your ways are best. Amen.

Happy Birthday Mom

And this I pray, that your love may abound still more and more in knowledge and all discernment, …
Philippians 1:9

It was Mom's 91st birthday. A day to celebrate. Janet and I decided to do something special for Mom. We planned a menu of all the tastes Mom remembered and loved. I made potato salad and coleslaw and bought some Noah Martin's summer sausage. I picked up some freshly baked rolls and some date-oatmeal cookies from a Mennonite bakery. Janet made a homemade pumpkin pie with real whipped cream. She also brought along some sweet dill pickles, paper plates, cutlery, apple juice, and cups. We were all set to surprise Mom.

"Oh Nancy, I'm so glad to see you. I'm feeling so abandoned," Mom said when we walked into her room.

Just then, one of the nurses came into Mom's room.

"Flo, you're finally awake. I heard your daughters are bringing you a nice birthday lunch. Why don't you put on some slacks? Either that or I could take mine off."

Mom laughed. So did I. I sure liked this nurse.

We'd planned on eating in the sunroom, but it was full, so we went to plan B and spread everything out on two TV trays in Mom's room. I filled Mom's plate with all her favourites. She was thrilled with the summer sausage and asked me to butter half the bun and made a huge fuss over it.

"Okay, Mom. Now try the potato salad and the coleslaw and the pickles."

"Oh no, I'm far too full to eat any more."

"Would you like some pumpkin pie with whipped cream, Mom?" Janet asked.

Mom brightened, took the piece of pie, and wolfed it down.

"Mom likes me best!" Janet said.

We howled. I could have saved myself a whole lot of trouble and just bought the summer sausage and buns. But Janet and I enjoyed feasting on what was left, so it wasn't a total loss.

Mom, with a full belly and a smile on her face, was asleep before we even left. Guess it takes a lot out of you when you turn 91. Happy Birthday dear Mama. We love you.

Celebrate Special Days

Birthdays only come once a year, and it doesn't take much to make it into a great party. If it's not possible to go out to celebrate, bring in some homemade or favourite food that the person you care for, enjoys. Remember, too, a little goes a long way! Enjoy the day and celebrate well.

Talking to God

Lord, I thank You for birthdays. Each one means You have protected me and given me life for another year. As Abraham Lincoln once said, "It's not the years in your life that counts, but it's the life in your years." May I use some of these precious moments to glorify You and be a friend and helper to those who need it most. Guide my steps I pray. Amen.

Noah Martin Summer Sausage

… be steadfast, immovable, always abounding in the work of the Lord, knowing that your labor is not in vain in the Lord.
1 Corinthians 15:58b

I know the Lord can use anything. Today He used summer sausage.

First thing this morning, I had a lovely breakfast with my cousin Karen at a local deli. Because we have the same relatives, stories, and memories, there was much to share. There's something special about families.

After Karen and I finished breakfast, I went to the counter and bought some fresh rolls and butter tarts and took them to Mom. When she saw me, she almost cried.

"Oh Nancy, you have no idea how unhappy I am!"

I listened to her as she tried her best to explain what was wrong.

"Wait and see what I brought you for lunch, Mom!" I tried to shift her thoughts to something pleasant.

She reluctantly sat on the couch with me while I opened up the summer sausage and the rolls I'd brought from home. She didn't think it looked good because everything was wrapped in butcher paper. I pulled a piece of summer sausage out, and she lit up like a Christmas tree. Her taste buds came alive when she ate piece after piece of Noah Martin's sausage. She didn't even want a roll with it.

"I just want to put it in my mouth and wrap my tongue around it," Mom said. Her eyes rolled heavenward as she continued to eat piece after piece of summer sausage.

"Oh Mom, I'm so glad you're enjoying every bite."

"I'm enjoying every chew!"

When I gave her some of my homemade chocolate covered fudge balls, her eyes rolled once more.

But I wasn't finished. I pulled out the butter tarts. She enjoyed every morsel.

After that, we both laid on her bed and began singing an old favourite chorus;

"When we all get to Heaven, what a day of rejoicing that will be. When we all see Jesus, we'll sing and shout the victory.[6]"

I felt like I had a taste of Heaven right there with the taste of butter tart on my lips and my happy mother lying beside me.

After a bit of a rest, Mom told me she wanted to share some of her goodies with Ken. We headed to his room and he, too, enjoyed some summer sausage and fudge balls. Mom became tired, so we walked back to her room arm in arm. I tucked her into bed and kissed her goodbye.

Another great memory. Thanks, Noah Martin, for helping make it happen!

It's the Little Things that Count

Time spent with the ones we love, or are responsible for, need not be difficult. Sometimes, all they truly want is for us to be with them, to hold their hand, to sing with them, or to read something that is meaningful to them. If you know a favourite food that would delight them, by all means give it to them, as long as it's something that is on their approved diet list. It will often make their day–and yours.

Talking to God

Father, I often need Your wisdom about what to do. Show me Your heart, for You alone know the one I care for and You understand her desires. May I be ever mindful of the honour I have of reaching out and helping someone who cannot help herself. Amen.

---

[6] Eliza E. Hewitt, 1851 - 1920.

Thanksgiving

Enter into His gates with thanksgiving,
And into His courts with praise. Be thankful
to Him and bless His name.
Psalm 100:4

I had so many reasons to be thankful. A huge part of my gratitude was for my precious family, Mom included. We were ready for our Dubrick Thanksgiving dinner. There would be twenty-six of us sitting around the long tables. My son, Nathan and his lovely wife, Tanya were hosting. David and I had built the entertainment-friendly home for ourselves many years ago. Now it was Nathan and Tanya's home, and we were truly thankful that they continued the tradition of opening their home to entertain family and friends.

Janet and Hank made arrangements to pick Mom up and take her to our Thanksgiving celebration.

"Hi Mom," Janet said, as she entered Mom's room.

Mom went to the phone, picked it up and said, "Hello?" At first, Janet didn't know if the phone had rung before she entered the room, so she was quiet at first. Mom said "Hello?" over and over. Janet finally interrupted.

"Hi Mom," she said again

"Where are you?" Mom said.

Janet had to chuckle. "Mom, I'm standing right here, in your room."

Mom still didn't look up until Janet went over to touch her gently on her arm. Mom jumped.

"Why are you playing tricks on me?" Mom said. "My mind is so bad that I can't even dress myself."

Janet told me that Mom was wearing a pretty flowered suit jacket and skirt. She pointed out to her how nice she looked. Mom touched her clothing and seemed surprised. Poor Mama.

Soon, Mom forgot about the fuss, though, and looked forward to being with us all. Janet got her ready and they were on their way.

It was good to see Mom walk in the door with Hank and Janet and soon we settled in for dinner.

We have a family tradition where we sing our blessing, "Praise God from Whom All Blessings Flow"[7] in four-part harmony before we eat. We stretch out the "Amen" because it's so beautiful.

That Thanksgiving was no exception. We dug in and feasted like there was no tomorrow! I sat beside Mom at the meal and she kept asking for more. She enjoyed my turkey with stuffing, gravy, and homemade cranberry sauce. And I loved watching her shovel it all in. Then, she spotted some homemade butter tarts and ate two in swift order. She saw another and gobbled that down too.

Later, as she was drinking her coffee, she said, "I hardly know anyone here."

I pointed out every family member individually and named them, but she didn't seem to recognize many and couldn't believe they were all her family. This saddened me greatly.

After we had finished gorging on turkey, with all the trimmings, the laughter continued and some played games while others rested.

Soon Mom had had enough, so Hank and Janet graciously left early to take her back to her room. We realized that it was confusing for her, but we wanted her to enjoy a good home-cooked turkey dinner. Looked like she enjoyed every bite!

I thought how she might have appreciated her quiet room a bit more after all the confusion of our large family gathering. I mean, we were a noisy bunch, but I sure loved every second of it. Turned out to be a gorgeous day all around.

---

[7] Composer (attributed to): Louis Bourgeois (1551); Source: Genevan Psalter, 1551; Public Domain

A Day Out Can Do a Lot of Good

Although it isn't always possible to take our charges out to someone's home for special days, it is usually worth the effort if we can find a way. Sometimes, the chaos of a large gathering can be intimidating and confusing for someone with dementia. Keep an eye on your loved one and remember, it doesn't need to be a long visit. Timing can make a difference to all concerned.

Talking to God

Lord, although I am thankful all year for Your many blessings, I happily set aside one day a year where I celebrate Your goodness together with friends and family. There aren't enough words to say, "Thank You," but I will try. You are good, and Your mercies endure forever. How blessed I am. Amen.

Little Things

Owe no one anything except to love one another, for he who loves another has fulfilled the law.
Romans 13:8

David was in Baltimore on business, so I was free to meet Janet. We had planned on taking Mom out for breakfast. We arrived at the restaurant, placed our orders, and within no time, the waitress brought us our food.

"Oh, is it ever nice to be served!" Mom said, taking a bite of her scrambled egg.

Janet and I looked at each other and burst out laughing.

"Mom, you're served every meal at Heritage House," Janet said.

Mom laughed at her statement and then dug in, like she hadn't eaten in weeks.

After we were finished, we were walking Mom out to Janet's car.

Mom said, "Well, this is the last time you'll have to take me out."

Janet and I glanced at each other.

"Okay, Mom," I said. She often says something like this every time we take her out—until cabin fever hits at Heritage House. Then comes her hint, "Didn't we used to go out for breakfast? I liked doing that!" And off we'd go again on another "breakfast adventure."

Making Memories

As we grow older, we realize that it's the little things in life that really count. The ordinary days that are full of love, tenderness, and laughter that make the world of difference. If we wait until we can do something really big, we'll miss out on the everyday miracles. Enjoy today to the fullest, even if it seems small.

Talking to God

"Lord, we thank You for this day. I am given a new beginning every morning, and it is up to me how I use it. Some days seem so humdrum and nothing special, but that could be because I am not looking. What I do in life counts, and although I should never be anxious, I can look for ways to do something, no matter how insignificant it may seem. You have blessed me, so please help me bless others. Amen.

Routines

And do not be conformed to this world, but be transformed by the renewing of your mind, that you may prove what is that good and acceptable and perfect will of God.
Romans 12:2

I, generally, love routines. There is something satisfying about knowing what is coming next and repeating it. However, sometimes even the best routines don't pan out. That's what happened on Sunday.

David and I usually visited Mom after church. Sometimes we took lunch along for the three of us. Other times we'd grab a quick bite first, or we'd meet up with friends for a long lunch and then pop in to see Mom after. We were consistent in our visits, although the times varied. It worked well and Mom seemed to appreciate our visits.

That particular Sunday, we had made lunch plans with a couple of friends. Turned out one of them took ill so they cancelled. I was disappointed, but as David and I were walking to the van after the service, I realized how very tired I was. David asked me what I wanted to do. I surprised myself by blurting out, "I just want to go home."

As we drove away, David agreed and mentioned that we could visit Mom the next day after hockey. It was settled. We ate the last of the turkey leftovers and both of us had a lovely Sunday afternoon nap. My lazy-bones attitude turned out to be a good thing. David and I both felt refreshed, and it seemed like Mom didn't even miss us! At least there was no call crying, "Where are you Nancy?" In that case, I was happy not to be missed.

Listen to Your Body

There may be times when you are just too weary to even think of doing something. That is perfectly fine. You need to take care of yourself. Caregivers can also get worn out, so if we don't take care of ourselves, we won't be able to take care of others. This is especially important to remember if we are the only caregiver. Set aside "me time" and don't feel guilty for doing it! Ask others to help fill in the gaps and then forget your troubles and enjoy your time away. You'll be much fresher afterward.

Talking to God

Oh God, sometimes I do things out of guilt, but that isn't Your plan. If I am truly motivated by love, and if You ordain it, things will fall into place and it will be glorious. If I try to do it in my own strength, I will fail every time, and it will be draining. Show me when to take a break and may I be a better person for it. Amen.

Romance

… for you are all one in Christ Jesus.
Galatians 3:28b

Our visit couldn't have gone better. The cleaning gal informed David and me that Mom was probably visiting Ken. We walked down to his room and lo and behold, there she was. Her face lit up when she saw us, but we had to listen to the old litany.

"Oh Nancy, you have no idea how difficult it is. I don't know which way is up and am so confused."

With a smile on my face I said, "I can help you out Mom."

I pointed to the ceiling. "This is up, and this is down." I pointed to the floor.

She didn't get it at first, but gave me a smile as my reward when it finally sunk in. Ken, on the other hand, seemed to recognize us and smiled when we talked to him. He was a delight. Mom lamented a little about how she longed to go to heaven, so we sang four songs about Heaven. Ken sang along. It was a grand time.

"Well thanks for coming," Mom said, after a while.

She said it three times in a row. David nudged me and whispered, "She wants us to leave."

I giggled and then kissed both of them goodbye. As we walked down the hall, we laughed at the irony of being dismissed, albeit politely.

Although Mom was happy for our visit, she realized it was good to be alone with Ken and was content. Goes to show you that romance is not dead—even when you're in your 90s.

Romance is Alive and Well

Although romance changes as we age, there is sometimes still a spark that never goes away. In my opinion, if there was a good deal of love and respect between a couple over the years, this makes for an even brighter spark. It is always a pleasure to see time-proven love between an elderly husband and wife and is something we can all strive for. Treat your spouse or special person with adoration, for we have no idea when it may slip away. And remember when you are caring for someone, he or she most likely had a past that you never knew about—loves and losses, joy and pain, highs and lows. All have a need for dignity, and we must give the respect that he or she deserves.

Talking to God

Father, I understand that life never stays the same. May I remember that even in the difficult times, You have a plan. Perhaps it's to get me ready for the future, or for growth for me now. Either way, my time is in Your hands and I am peaceful with that knowledge. Amen.

Extra Special Breakfast

He who dwells in the secret place of the Most High
Shall abide under the shadow of the Almighty.
Psalm 91:1

It was a cold, rainy day, but Mom was really looking forward to Janet and me taking her out for breakfast. We made sure we wore long sleeves and took umbrellas for the outing. We met at Heritage House. Mom was in the hallway waiting for us. That was a shock. Usually she was in bed asleep or at least resting, getting ready for the big adventure. It was nice to see her this excited. She wasn't dressed warmly enough, though, so I helped her put on something more appropriate. Soon Janet arrived and we were on our way.

I'd been up since 5:00 a.m. so I was hungry. Breakfast was delicious.

"I could make a breakfast out of this meal!" Mom said, digging in right away, intent on consuming every crumb. She looked over at my plate

"Why didn't they give me eggs too?"

I reached over, moved her toast, and, there were two eggs over-easy smiling up at her. Mom was glad and gobbled up her eggs with gusto.

Janet was allergic to eggs, so her choices were limited. She had toast and jam and a fruit cup but would have loved our breakfast. I felt it only right that I share some of my bacon, but Mom ate hers greedily.

"Ouch"

Mom bit her tongue. Janet and I both asked, "Are you alright Mom?"

Her answer was cute. "It's okay, I still have my tongue."

At one point, Mom said something and asked Janet, "Isn't that right?" Janet simply answered with a *yes*. I hadn't understood what Mom said, so I asked Janet. Her response was, "Not sure, but I thought I'd agree."

Just before we left the restaurant, Mom said, "I didn't have any accidents here, right?"

Janet and I laughed, and I said, "No Mom. That's why we are welcomed back."

She laughed and felt mighty pleased with herself. When I helped her back to her room, she saw the beverage cart in the hall and asked for a ginger ale and quickly downed it in a few gulps. Then she asked if I'd fill the glass with cold water and she drank quite a lot of that too. Obviously, eating a big breakfast made you thirsty.

Kindness Matters

I love this quote from Leo Buscagla: "Too often we underestimate the power of a touch, a smile, a kind word, and a listening ear, an honest compliment, or the smallest act of caring, all of which have the potential to turn a life around." We never know when our kindness will mean the most, so spread your love and kindness wherever and whenever you are able.

Talking to God

Lord, You have given each one of us the ability to be kind. It doesn't cost me anything, or intrude on my life, but rather it enriches both the giver and the receiver. It has been said that kindness is the hardest thing to give away, because it keeps coming back to us. May I never miss a chance to be kind. Amen.

Mom Goes to RIM Park

… Lord God of Israel, there is no God in heaven above or on earth below like You, who keep Your covenant and mercy with Your servants who walk before You with all their hearts.
1 Kings 8:23b

Ever since David started to play hockey at a local indoor sports complex in the summer, Mom had wanted to see it. She was especially curious when I told her I walked on the track there, while he played hockey with the guys.

Today was the day. I tried to call Mom twice but received no answer, so I took a chance. After dropping David off at RIM, I drove to Heritage House to see if she wanted to join us.

When I arrived, Mom was in bed, which wasn't unusual. I touched her gently. She opened her eyes and saw me.

"Oh Nancy," she wailed. "I am at the end of my rope!"

I tried to soothe her as she repeated her teary tirade.

As gently as I could I said, "Mom, would you like an adventure today?"

"Anything to get out of here!" she said.

I explained, briefly, that we were going to the sports complex to walk on the track and then we would have an indoor picnic. She seemed happy with the plan. I got her ready and off we went.

As soon as we walked through the front door of the expansive complex, Mom was completely overwhelmed. I don't know if she'd ever seen such a huge building before. Her confusion intensified, the farther we walked. Mom looked down the long halls.

"Oh Nancy, now I'm going to worry that you'll get lost!"

I tried to reassure her that I knew this place inside and out and would never get lost. But my words didn't calm her much.

"I'm going to have nightmares now."

Mom continued to be anxious, and it surprised me. I had figured she would have been pleased to see where I walked a few times a week, but instead it overwhelmed her.

It wasn't exactly going quite the way I had pictured it. I talked Mom into walking a little further. When we walked by the Pro Shop, she asked what it was. I told her that it was where customers could buy outfits for figure skaters and they also sharpened and sold skates there.

"Well I sure wouldn't buy anything there!"

Guess you'll have to buy your skates and figure skating outfits elsewhere, Mom.

Mom noticed the picnic basket and was anxious to eat, so I settled her down, bought us each a cup of tea and we dug in. I'd made egg-salad sandwiches (I make a mean egg-salad) but she didn't say much. The homemade pickled beets were well received, but I'd used her recipe, so no wonder she liked them. The real highlight was when I brought out some chocolate wafer cookies. Her eyes lit up. She ate at least five of them in quick succession.

Guess I could have saved myself a lot of trouble and just brought the store-bought cookies, but who knew?

Later, we went back to Heritage House and I signed her in and kissed her goodbye. Then I drove back to the sports complex. David joined me at the table after his hockey game.

"How was it?" he asked.

I told him what happened.

"Never again," I said.

"Well at least you tried," David said. "Your mom doesn't always realize what she's doing, but you thought she'd like it. Chalk it up to experience."

He was right. Sometimes you win and sometimes you lose. At least it was an adventure and it gave me something to write about. Just hope Mom doesn't have nightmares!

Sometimes It's a Sigh Day

It is discouraging when things don't go as planned, isn't it? We may have great anticipation of what the day should be and how the person we're trying to please will react, only to have it blow up in our faces. Times like this make us want to quit, but that's not the right response. We should learn from the fiasco and remember not to repeat it. Even so, perhaps a similar plan may work once the person is in a better state of mind. Don't give up.

Talking to God

Oh Father. Life can be so discouraging sometimes. I try, but it falls flat. However, I know that I disappoint You time and time again, yet You never give up on me. You forgive me when I confess, and You wipe my slate clean and I carry on. May I forgive easily and quickly and not hold any grudges. Help me remember that sometimes my human brain just doesn't grasp some situations and there's nothing anyone can do. I entrust it all to Your loving hands. Amen.

Early Morning Phone Call

And let us not grow weary while doing good, for in due season we shall reap if we do not lose heart.
Galatians 6:9

"Good morning Mom!"

"Oh Nancy, I can't handle it. I think I'm having a stroke, and no one is doing anything about it!"

"I'm sure it's not that bad."

"Oh yes, it is!"

"Well, I guess I'll have to phone Janet to cancel the breakfast at our favourite restaurant that we had planned."

There was a long pause. I waited because I sensed Mom was thinking.

"Well, I think I would be up to that," Mom said, suddenly changing her attitude.

The change made me smile. It's interesting how a little bribe like a restaurant breakfast would suddenly make her all better.

When David, Janet, and I arrived in her room, Mom was neatly dressed, with her hair combed and her teeth in, ready to go. She was thrilled to be going out and soon we had our coffee at the restaurant. It tasted good.

Mom mentioned that the staff was fussing over her earlier. She wondered why.

"Well, Mom, I think it's because they knew that your lovely, beautiful, and charming daughters were taking you out for breakfast."

"Well I think you're stretching it," she said as she was drinking her coffee. "I needed a stiff coffee this morning!"

Her comment reminded us of the time she and Ken were in a store in Florida one morning. Mom was, apparently, thirsty and needed some water.

"Take me out of here. I need a drink really bad!" she had said rather loudly to Ken.

We can imagine that the other shoppers looked at Ken with sympathy, since he was obviously married to a lush who needed a *drink* so early in the day! We all had a good laugh when Ken relayed that story to us many years ago.

Mom was always happy when we talked about times past, especially the funny stories. It was a lovely breakfast, but when the cheque came, it was clear she needed help.

"Uh-oh, I have cramps," she said to me.

That's all I needed to hear. As I walked her to the bathroom she kept saying, "Oh dear, hurry! Oh dear, hurry!"

I helped Mom into a stall and no sooner had she sat down, I realized it really was a close call. I couldn't help it; I laughed and I laughed. Mom soon joined in.

"Better out than in I always say," came the sage advice from a lady in the next stall."

That made Mom and me laugh even more.

On our way out, Mom asked, "Did I leave anything behind?" I chuckled and said, "Just what was important, Mom."

We were still laughing when we got back to the table. I explained what had happened to Janet so she could join in with the girl giggles.

Janet took us on a scenic route as she drove us around so we could see the pretty trees. Before long, Mom was happy to go back to her room and climb into bed.

Seniors Say the Cutest Things

Journal or jot down funny, cute, or insightful things you hear in your travels. You'll be surprised how many of them can bring a smile to your face, laughter, or warm memories for years to come. We sometimes forget how important the little things are. Too often, we get burdened down with the humdrum of life. Ask God to remind you of important or interesting happenings during the day, if it is appropriate, or store them in a computer file, a journal, in a scrapbook, or a special memory box.

Talking to God

Father, You made sure that the disciples carefully and faithfully kept record of many of the miracles of the life of Jesus when He was on earth. This means I am able to get a glimpse of You. Remind me that I, too, have stories to record and I thank You for the technology that allows me to do just that. Give me wisdom and insight into how to document them all. Amen.

Childhood Memory

For we do not wrestle against flesh and blood, but against principalities, against powers, against the rulers of the darkness of this age, against spiritual hosts of wickedness in the heavenly places.
Ephesians 6:12

My first memory of Mom was when I was about four years old and living with my parents and my older sister, Janet, who was about seven. My Uncle Jack (who I adored) drove a delivery truck at the time. One day he asked Mom if he could take me on one of his short runs. Mom agreed and I was eagerly looking forward to it. However, before he arrived, I must have been a bad little girl, so as punishment, she told me I could not go.

I was upset at this news and realized Uncle Jack would be there shortly. Because he would have to leave without me, I did what I thought was best all around. I promptly laid on the floor and had a temper tantrum. I kicked, screamed, and cried, but Mom would not budge. Sure enough, Uncle Jack came and left with his lovely truck and all I got out of the whole ordeal was a sore throat and sore heels from kicking and screaming. Although I couldn't recall what I did wrong for Mom to punish me that way, the fact remained, she was right in doing so. I learned a lesson that day. Tantrums didn't work and to my knowledge, I never did have another one. Good job, Mom!

Years later, the roles were reversed, but I could not punish Mom because of her misdeeds, for she was unaware of her "tantrums." It was the same … but different.

Hang our Heads

We can all look back and wonder why we did some of the things we did as children. Not one of us was a perfect child. In fact, not one of us turned into perfect adults or parents. We need to give ourselves some slack for our faults and failures, for we all have them. However, it is always good to ask God to help us grow and learn from those mistakes.

Talking to God

How thankful I am that You never turn me away when I come to You. Sometimes it is for a problem that I have over and over and can't seem to get past, and other times it's for things I should have done but didn't. Thank You for loving me no matter what. Help me to learn from You as I carry on in life. Amen.

Hard on Myself

But You, Oh Lord, are a shield for me,
My glory and the One who lifts up my head.
Psalm 3:3

Although I truly enjoyed writing a devotional, I realized it was far different than writing my posts on social media. As I was typing, I would sometimes hear a little voice in my head; "That is stupid! Whatever gave you the idea you could write? No one will want to read it and no editor would ever publish your drivel!"

It was a battle and a challenge to feel any kind of inspiration with those thoughts rumbling around. So, I confided in Glynis.

"This is not uncommon, but you need to ignore those ugly voices and keep on writing," she said.

So, that's what I did. My life had been full of adventures. I never seemed to run out of stories. My mother was a huge influence on me growing up and I truly wanted to share her life with whoever would listen.

My mom was such an interesting character (even if she didn't believe it) and she had been a great role model. Over the years she showed her three girls how to face trials with peace, laughter, and a hearty trust in God. She told us that He would always see us through. Those kinds of thoughts helped. I carried on and decided to do the best job I could manage. Fingers to keyboard, it was; ignoring those pesky little voices who really didn't know what they were talking about anyway, was good advice.

Doubting Ourselves

We all have doubts and question our own abilities from time to time, but we should never camp there. It's not bad to be reminded that we are imperfect, but to put ourselves down is an upside-down form of pride. We need not think lowly of ourselves. Instead it is better to rather think little of ourselves and more of others. True fulfillment comes when we reach out to others to do what God has designed for us to do—faults and all.

Talking to God

I am all too aware of my shortcomings, Father. Sometimes they are glaring, but thankfully, You look beyond my faults and see the diamond in the rough in me. May I not dwell on negative emotions, but simply listen and obey Your direction. There are some who need me, and I want to be Your hand extended. Amen.

Precious Memories

Every good gift and every perfect gift is from above, …
James 1:17a

After church, David and I went out for lunch with four dear friends and enjoyed good food and lots of laughs. After we said our goodbyes, David and I went to visit another dear friend in a retirement home and then carried on to Heritage House to visit Mom. It was a surprise that Mom wasn't napping in her room. It was 3:30 p.m. by the time David and I had arrived. We wondered if she might have been in Ken's room. What we saw was heartwarming.

Ken was in his lazy-boy chair as usual, and Mom was sitting on the seat of his walker. They were holding hands. Mom's eyes were closed. We crept in so we wouldn't disturb them. "Oh Ken, how I wish it were time to go to bed," Mom said. "I'm so tired. We both need a lot of sleep you know. Oh, but I'm tired. Don't you wish it was time to go to bed?"

Funny thing is, Ken was wide awake, stroking her hand, and didn't seem the least bit sleepy.

We did not want to disturb either one of them, so I just sat on the bed and watched. David found a chair and settled in. Soon Mom opened her eyes and a huge smile came on her face when she saw it was us. Of course, she asked how long we'd been there. I told her what I'd heard and we both laughed.

Ken tried to get up out of his chair, but he was struggling. Mom gently chided him. "Ken, you shouldn't try to get out of your chair by yourself. Why don't you just sit back and relax? David and Nancy are here."

"Whenever I do something wrong, I don't mind if you tell me." he said as clear as day.

We were impressed.

"Usually Ken is just a quiet little mouse," Mom said to us. Then she turned to Ken.

"Right, Honey?"

Ken laughed and said, “Well, even a quiet little mouse can get mighty loud from time to time.”

I burst out laughing.

“Ken, you made a joke,” I said and repeated it to him. He gave a hearty belly laugh—something I hadn’t seen in years—and we all kept laughing.

Then just like that, Ken sat back in his chair. I could see the door of his eyes shut down and he lost what we were just enjoying. Dementia is an awful disease and it robs people of so much, but for one brief moment, we had our old Ken back.

It was apparent that Mom really couldn’t stay awake any longer, so we walked her down to her room. I tucked her into bed and we quietly left. I’m so glad we witnessed the love between the two of them and then a short glimpse of how things used to be. Very precious.

Nice Memories

Treasure the good times. They may be few and far between, but when they do come, do not skip over them. Rather, savour the beauty of the moment. These are what will keep you going through the hard times. Celebrate small victories for what they are—victories. You’ll feel lighter and will be given more energy when you do.

Talking to God

Father. How I adore You. I know that I do not deserve all the good things I have, for I tend to either take them for granted, or not see them for what they are—good and perfect gifts. May I celebrate whatever little victories I experience and trust You to help me through the hard times. Amen.

Toothless

But above all these things put on love,
which is the bond of perfection.
Colossians 3:14

Mom lost her dentures, poor dear. I found out when I called her Tuesday morning.

"When I went to sleep my teeth were on my bedside table, and when I woke up, they were gone!"

I asked if the staff were aware of it. Mom said that they had checked everywhere too and couldn't find them. I waited until 4:00 that afternoon to see if the lost had been found. Alas, it wasn't to be.

The following day, we stopped in and saw Mom wandering the halls, toothless. In the past, she wouldn't have dared to be seen without her teeth. With a sinking heart, I knew they were gone. David and I did a thorough room search, just in case. He checked the cushions on the couch, down the sides of the lazy-boy chair, and under all the other furniture, but no teeth. How frustrating!

We asked the staff to check Mom's neighbour to see if they were in her room. This lady often came into Mom's room and ordered her to get out of her room. We've seen her do it, so perhaps she was the culprit.

This was not our first encounter with missing teeth. I thought back to the episode with my grandmother.

It happened many years ago, also in a nursing home. Grandma ran down the hallway in the nursing home with her hand over her mouth, gagging. A concerned nurse intervened.

"Emma, what's wrong?"

Grandma had pointed to her mouth. "Teeth."

The nurse asked, "What about your teeth Emma?"

"Not mine!"

Grandma's quick comeback had been a classic!

We were hoping no one else was wearing Mom's teeth. We asked the staff what happened in these cases and they assured us that their denturists would make house calls. It wouldn't be too hard getting her a new set. First, we needed to find out where she got them made, originally. She'd had dentures for many years, so we didn't know if she'd even remember.

She tried hard to recall where she had got them, but she just couldn't remember. Then suddenly, she blurted out, "Dr. Rush!"

Now we were getting somewhere. We called Dr. Rush's office and found out that Mom remembered correctly. She did get her teeth there. But it was far too long ago for them to be of any help. There were little or few records. The receptionist gave us the name of a company to call. We were hopeful we could set up an appointment for someone to come into the nursing home to fit her for new dentures.

Lost and Found

We all know that clarity will come in extraordinary ways with those we care for. When it does, everyone feels happy. We must remember that sometimes even our own brains don't work the way we'd like. Sad commentary, but true! Rejoice in the times when clarity occurs.

Talking to God

Oh Lord. There are times when things happen that throw me for a loop, but I thank You that You have the answer if I am quiet and open to hear Your voice. May I not get frustrated but look at every possible way to solve a problem. Sometimes it's an easy fix, and sometimes it isn't, but please help me to take one step at a time. Amen.

Answer on the Way

He has shown you, O man, what is good; And what does the Lord require of you But to do justly, To love mercy, And to walk humbly with your God?
Micah 6:8

It's hard to have dignity without teeth. Although Mom was thrilled to see us, she could not help but mourn the loss of her teeth. She wondered, again, if someone took them. I mentioned that perhaps she threw them out accidently. She was adamant that this was not the case. I asked her if she remembered wrapping them up in a tissue and suggested she could have tossed them.

"I'd feel the difference in the tissue if my bulky teeth would be in it, and I would know immediately," she said.

"I treasure my teeth and am very careful with them."

I acknowledged that, yes, she was careful with her teeth. But something had happened to them. When I talked to the staff, they told us that they were still on the lookout for them. Although we were all sad, Mom did say something that made David and me laugh.

"There's one woman that I'm suspicious of at my table. I think maybe she's the culprit."

Mom was dead serious.

"I watch her mouth carefully to see how she's doing with my teeth."

Mom wasn't trying to be funny, but it felt good to lighten the atmosphere a little. Even she laughed when we did.

The staff were concerned that since she lost her teeth, she hadn't been eating very well, so the nutritionist changed her to a soft diet. It seemed to have made a difference. We arranged for a denturist to come in to make a mold for a new set of teeth for Mom. David and I planned to be there with her, for moral support, if nothing else. I wasn't looking forward to it, for I knew it would be difficult for Mom to have that *goop* put in her mouth for the mold. I've had it done, and it was tough because of my sensitive gag reflex. At the time, I was afraid I would throw up all over myself and the dental hygienist. Knowing Mom, I figured it would probably upset her, too.

Of course, the denturist is a professional and obviously deals with seniors all the time. We decided that our best approach until it happened, was to love and support her as much as we could. (And then, rejoice when she finally got her new teeth!)

Outside Help Needed

Sometimes we think we can "do it alone," but that is pride talking and it can cause great damage to ourselves. There's nothing wrong with admitting we cannot do some things on our own, for that allows others to step in and feel that they are needed. None of us is an island. We need each other. You'll never know the friendships that can evolve because of it. Could be very good indeed!

Talking to God

When Jesus walked on the earth, I am reminded that He chose twelve disciples to walk alongside Him. We all need each other Father, and sometimes it can be difficult to admit. Needing help is not announcing failure. Rather it is saying that I am only human. Show me when I can do it on my own, and when I need help. Give me the humility to accept it with thanksgiving. Amen.

Mom is on Her Way to New Teeth!

You will keep him in perfect peace,
Whose mind is stayed on You,
Because he trusts in You.
Isaiah 26:3

The denturist was scheduled to come to Mom's room at 4:15 p.m., so we made sure we were there ahead of time. When David came with me, I always went into Mom`s room first. One never knew what state of undress she could be in. That day she was in bed wearing only her underwear. I woke her up and quickly got her dressed and combed her hair so she would be ready for her appointment. Shortly after, a handsome young man walked in and introduced himself as Jason. Mom couldn't quite understand what was going to happen, but Jason was very kind and gentle, explaining everything he was going to do as he took the impression for the new dentures. Although I had to interpret everything he said, Mom was wonderful and cooperated well.

I was dreading the part where the metal tray with the *goop* on it would be put into her mouth. She did gag twice at first, but I stood beside her and stroked her back. I spoke lovingly to her and miraculously, she settled right down. She didn't like when he had to loosen it and pull it out, though, but that was only a few seconds.

The bottom plate was much easier, and I was relieved. Mom had the pink *goop* on her lips which she didn't like, but Jason wiped it off and she felt better. At one point when the small tray and *goop* was in her mouth, Jason asked Mom to stick her tongue out. She did.

"Mom, that wasn't nice of you to stick your tongue out at Jason," I said, trying to lighten the mood. "You taught us never to stick our tongue out at anyone."

David jumped in. "He asked for it, I heard him. It was Jason`s fault." We all laughed.

I was relieved that the worst part was over. Soon Mom would be able to smile again, eat solid food, and regain her dignity.

Worrying Isn't Helpful

It's always a relief to have a difficult procedure over and done. Sometimes, (like in my case), I worried needlessly for Mom, who turned out to be a real trouper. Worry is a mighty useless activity, and not only does it hurt us but is a waste of time. Do you ever worry about something coming up, only to find it wasn't nearly as bad as you'd thought? God does say that He will give us peace, but we must accept it.

Talking to God

Oh Father, sometimes I carry on and worry as if You are not with me every step of the way. Forgive me when I take burdens of the future, when there is nothing that can be accomplished by doing so. Teach me to take one day at a time, and one step at a time. Amen.

A Very Bad, Not So Good Day

The Lord will perfect that which concerns me;
Your mercy, O Lord, endures forever; Do not forsake the works of Your hands.
Psalm 138:8

Mom had a meltdown. David and I were out running errands for most of the day, so I wasn't so sure when Mom left the long, tearful message on our answering machine. We didn't get home until late that day. I did notice the light on the answering machine flashing but was anxious to get supper started so I figured I'd check the messages once I got things going. However, I forgot until 9:30 that night and felt horrible when I finally listened to her message. It had been quite a while since I'd heard Mom sobbing and moaning and it broke my heart.

"Nancy, you have to help me. I can't look after Ken, and no one knows how to look after me," she cried. "I can't take it anymore and feel so alone. No one cares here and I need you. I think I'll just get out of here and walk away and no one will hear from me again. Please help me Nancy."

She repeated her concerns and I felt awful that I hadn't listened to the message as soon as we got home.

It was too late to call, so I made sure I phoned her first thing the next morning. I dialed. No answer. I called her after breakfast. Still no answer. By 11:30 a.m. I made one last call to her room. If she didn't pick up, I decided I would call the nursing station, but this time she cheerfully answered on the third ring. I asked if she was sleeping.

"No Nancy, I wasn't sleeping. I was just looking through my drawers looking for some chocolate to give to Ken. I couldn't find any, but that's okay, because it's almost time for lunch anyway."

Relief flooded through me and soon we were talking about the weather and other mundane things.

"When do you think Janet and you are going to take me out for breakfast again? I do love that so much you know."

"How about next Tuesday?" I suggested. "Would that work for you?"

"Oh, that would be wonderful. Just call ahead and tell me so that I have something to look forward to."

I didn't say anything about the meltdown. She had obviously forgotten it. I was most thankful that she had. I never knew from moment to moment what triggered the drama for Mom, but at least there were good times in between, and we were thankful for each and every one.

Don't Give Up

There are times when we think no one sees the sacrifice we make day after day for those we care for, but God does. Be encouraged today that your good deeds and patience do count.

Talking to God

God, I know that You are all powerful. You promise to be my defender, my deliverer, my refuge in trouble, my God of mercy. Oh, what peace this gives. Thank You for all You do for me. May I be ever mindful of these truths. Amen.

Another Meltdown

O Lord God of hosts, Who is mighty like You, O Lord? Your faithfulness also surrounds You. You rule the raging of the sea; When its waves rise, You still them.
Psalm 89:8-9

The call came while I was elbow deep in the mess of canning pickled beets. Anyone who works with beets knows what a challenge pickling them can be. But I'd had the large bag of beets for a while, so I knew that Saturday had to be "Pickled Beets Day." I'd put it off long enough. I'd already made the pickle juice and was sterilizing the jars. The beets were almost cooked when the phone rang. One of the nurses called to say Mom was having a difficult time and wondered if I'd be willing to talk to her. Of course, I'd said yes, and Mom got on the phone.

"I think I'll walk out of this place and no one will hear from me again. No one cares about me and I'm all alone. It is unbearable!" Mom's cries were pitiful. I listened for a while.

"Mom, how can you say no one cares?" I said, gently. "The nurse who made the call for you was very kind and gentle and she cared enough to call me."

Mom didn't have anything to say to that but wondered if I could come and help her anyway. I explained that I was pickling beets and could not leave the process.

"Oh Nancy, what I wouldn't give to sit at your kitchen table and watch you pickle beets," she said. "I wouldn't say a word!"

I knew Mom would enjoy getting out, but I also needed to be practical and had to tell her that it wasn't going to work out.

"Mom, please understand, but I can't leave right now, and David is working. Besides, you wouldn't be able to manage our outside stairs. I'm so sorry."

Mom calmed down and I was able to talk her into lying down for a nice nap, so we said our goodbyes and I hoped all was well. A bit later, I called the same nurse and asked her how

Mom was doing. She told me that Mom settled right down and was happy once again and even visited Ken after her nap. The nurse even overheard Mom say to Ken," I talked to Nancy and all is well." Thank You Lord!

Feeling Helpless

There are times when we simply cannot help those for whom we deeply care. As long as they are in good hands, we must trust those in charge and do our best to talk them down if we are able. No need for feeling guilty, for that doesn't do any good. Just rest in the fact that you are doing your very best.

Talking to God

Dear Jesus. How often I wish I could be two places at once, but I can't. However, You are not bound by time and space, so You can be everywhere at once. I stand in awe of Your power and are ever so thankful for that truth. You see my loved ones and know exactly what they are going through and love them more than I could ever possibly understand. Give me peace when I am unable to help, and simply rest in the knowledge that You are there with them and with me. Amen.

Memories

Wilfred and Florence Dubrick on their wedding day, 1945

The Dubrick Family Singers, 1963
(Back Row, left to right) Janet, Wilfred, Nancy,
and Jane in the front.

The Dubrick Sisters
(Left to Right, Back Row) Janet, Nancy,
and Jane in the front.

1954

Front Row: (Left to Right) Nancy Dubrick, Wayne Leis, Bob Litwiller, Janet Dubrick, Gloria Litwiller
2nd Row: Ron Litwiller
3rd Row: (Left to Right) Grandma Emma Litwiller, Grandpa Herb Litwiller, Florence (Mom) Dubrick, Wilfred (Dad) Dubrick, Doris Leis, Elmer Leis
4th Row: Joyce Kranz, Len Litwiller, Barb Litwiller, Jim Litwiller (baby), Vietta Litwiller, Stan Litwiller, Rita Litwiller, Art Litwiller

Florence and Ken Kufske, 2005.

The Dubrick Girls. 2013
Janet, Florence (Mom), Nancy, Jane

Which Way is Up?

Many waters cannot quench love,
Nor can the floods drown it.
Song of Solomon 8:7a

I made sure to make Mom a batch of my famous fudge and when David and I visited, we gave it to her.

"I do love our family recipe for fudge. Isn't it the best Nancy?" said Mom.

"I totally agree Mom, it is the best!"

She rolled her eyes with delight as she sucked on a piece. We could see that she was tired, so we eventually took the hint. After she had finished her fudge, we said goodbye and quietly left so she could have a nap. We were thankful that all was well.

Then early evening, a nurse called to tell us that Mom was beside herself. She put Mom on the phone.

"Nancy, I don't know which way is up," she cried. "Can you tell me what I'm supposed to do?"

I asked her what she wanted to do, but she kept telling me she didn't know. I tried to give her lots of ideas, but she rejected everything I suggested. I hinted she could go to bed for the night. She liked that idea, so that's what she did.

Such are the joys of dementia. I can't imagine what Mom goes through during these times, but I am thankful that she usually snaps out of them quickly. I only wish I could settle down as quickly after her calls!

Help, I Need Wisdom Here

Oh, for the wisdom of Solomon! There are times when we simply do not have the answers and that causes us to be more stressed. Those we care for often forget that they've dumped on us, and then we must deal with the fallout. However, we must remember that we are committed to this and we don't need to feel guilty.

Talking to God

God You promised to be my burden bearer. There are times when the load feels so heavy and it's hard for me to carry on. Give me Your wisdom and show me how to deal with the stress in a good way and simply leave it at Your feet and carry on. Thank You that Your shoulders are strong enough for me to lean on and then You can help to carry my burden. Amen.

Reinforcement Arrives

… and let us run with endurance the race
that is set before us, …
Hebrews 12:1c

Janet was home! I knew that we depended on each other to help Mom but having her gone for two tumultuous weeks, made me realize just how much I did depend on her. Hank and Janet had been visiting their daughter and family in Tennessee, but now my sister was back to help carry some of the load, and I was relieved.

Since her return, Janet had paid a few visits to Mom. She had been anxious to see how she was doing. When we talked on the phone, she gave me the rundown of her visits. Apparently, the first time, instead of being glad to see her returning daughter, Mom wailed about how much she hated it in the nursing home and wondered why she was still living. It wasn't a pleasant visit, Janet told me. Bravely, she went again the following day and found out that Mom had called Hank earlier. Janet had been out with friends, so she was unaware of the call. Mom had wailed and wailed to Hank about things until he had to gracefully close the conversation and say goodbye.

Janet did not know about the call and innocently ventured into the lion's den. Mom had been eating lunch when she arrived and although she'd calmed down a little bit from her tirade with Hank, she was still an unhappy camper for a while. Janet knew what to do. She took her to her room, gave her some chocolate, and they ended up having a nice time singing hymns.

Mom did tell Janet she was concerned about a few things.

"When is David going to get my teeth for me?" was her biggest concern. "It's taking forever," she said, "and I don't understand why."

We smiled every time she said that. For some reason, Mom had it in her head that not only did David set the procedure up to get her new dentures to be made, he was the one making them!

She was convinced this was right and no amount of explaining would change her mind.

So, come on David. Get off your duff and make those teeth already. Mom needs them!

Help Each Other

There's an old German saying, "When one is helping the other, both are strong." Do you have someone you can call upon to help carry your load? If not, pray that God will guide you to someone who would walk beside you and give you a helping hand when you need it.

Talking to God

God, there are times when I simply need another person to help with the load. Often, I hate to even ask, but I could be robbing someone else of a blessing by trying to carry it all by myself. Show me who I can reach out to so we can walk together on this journey. Amen.

Mama in Quarantine

I will lift up my eyes to the hills – From whence comes my help? My help comes from the Lord,
Who made heaven and earth.
Psalm 121:1-2

David and I were surprised to see Mom in her room with a tray of food in front of her when we arrived just before 1:00 in the afternoon. My heart ached as I saw her slumped in her lazy-boy chair with her food, untouched. Then we found out she had a cold and a cough, so they were serving all meals in her room until she was better. We noticed the sign on the front door stating that there was a quarantine and children were not permitted (I wondered if the sign meant me.) I went in anyway. They were obviously taking precautions.

I woke Mom up and told her it was lunch time. I sat in front of her and tried to encourage her to eat some soup. But she only took a few sips, and just tasted a bit of the jellied salad that was on her dinner tray. The rest of the solids sat untouched, but she did drink her milk, some ginger ale, and water, so that was good.

We told her about a poverty simulation we'd just presented to 56 grade four students at a school in Cambridge, but she was lethargic, so we didn't say too much. Mom began dozing off in her chair, so I moved the tray away and tried to help her get to bed for a nap, but she didn't have the strength. I tucked the blanket carefully around her and fluffed the little pillow by her head and gave her a kiss on the forehead and quietly slipped out of the room. I just left her sleeping there because she looked comfortable.

We Get Weary Also

Sometimes it feels as if an Arctic wind has blown in, and we shiver in the cold. We feel inadequate to help the ones we are taking care of and stand by helplessly. However, we know One who sticks closer than a brother and is there 24/7–even when we can't be. Lean heavily on the Saviour, for He is our burden bearer.

Talking to God

Father, I need You. I need You in the good times and when things seem to be out of my control. I need Your peace, Your comfort, and Your healing power. Thank You that You never turn me away, but You welcome me with Your Presence. I rely heavily on You. Amen.

No Germs Through Phonelines

Come to Me, all you who labor and are heavy laden,
and I will give you rest.
Matthew 11:28

I was trying hard to be thankful during my lingering illness. There was an especially bad cold bug going around and it latched on to me. I can't recall how long it had been since I felt this bad. Not only that, I couldn't visit Mom and that was difficult. But I really did try to be positive and thankful.

One of the things I was thankful for was the telephone. I may not always have been able to visit Mom during my illness, but we could talk, and we usually found something to laugh at.

"No germs can get through the phonelines," one of us would say, then we would both have a chuckle.

But even over the phone I could tell that the dementia was getting worse. That broke my heart. I'd been concerned because she'd fallen twice. Mom's memory was sketchy, and she didn't make sense with many of her sentences. This concerned me greatly, but I was powerless to do anything because of my illness.

While I was sick, Janet had been taking my shifts. After her second fall, Mom hurt her wrist. Janet said it was swollen and she let me know that Heritage House had arranged for her to get an x-ray. Turned out there was no break, just a sprain. Although a sprain was still not pleasant, we were glad it wasn't broken.

For a while the staff kept Mom in her room and served her meals on a tray, because she was showing a slight fever. When I called her on the phone later and asked her if she was able to walk down to the dining room for her meals, her answer saddened me.

"You know, I'm not sure."

She hadn't shown that level of confusion before, so it was difficult to hear. We were so thankful that she still knew Janet and me and our husbands, though. I was glad to hear that she remembered that I often walked at the sports complex. She even recalled that I took her there for a visit a while back.

When We're Down for the Count

It can be mighty rough when the caregiver is down. We are used to being the strong one, at the ready when needed. But then sickness drops by for a visit, the rug is pulled out, and we are flat on our backs. We can be at peace, though, even though we are unable to visit or care for our loved one because it would be far worse to spread our germs to them and everyone else. Best thing is to relax, drink lots of liquids, and sleep. Soon we'll be right as rain and able to help once again. Use this time to heal.

Talking to God

You who made me, know that I am weak and sometimes down for the count for a while because of illness. You also know that perhaps I needed to be 'set aside' to rest and regroup. Help me to simply accept my limitations and concentrate on getting well again, trusting that I am not indispensable. Amen.

Mama is Declining

But now, O Lord, You are our Father;
We are the clay, and You our potter;
And all we are the work of Your hand.
Isaiah 64:8

I was still struggling with my health, but I tried my best to keep calling Mom every morning. The other day when I called, I thought perhaps I woke her.

"Is it morning already?" Her voice sounded groggy.

I apologized for waking her up.

"Oh no, you didn't wake me. I've been up already for I'm all dressed. I just climbed back into bed until breakfast."

That made me feel better.

"Did you get dressed by yourself or did someone come and assist you?" Her answer caused my heart to sink.

"I'm not sure."

Likely it would have been ten minutes earlier that she was helped into her clothes, yet she couldn't remember. The reality of what was happening to Mom was weighing heavily on me, and I felt helpless to do anything about it.

Having family visit had always been important to Mom. She often lamented that she only felt comfortable with family members and loved when any of us visited. So, when she couldn't remember that her sister Gloria along with her husband Earl visited her, I again felt overwhelmingly sad. She didn't even remember that Janet visited a day ago. That was unusual.

It is interesting though that Mom remembered that I was not well and was concerned about me. She understood that I could not go and see her because of the possible threat of me spreading germs. Thankfully she was content to talk on the phone, yet she couldn't recall if she got herself dressed or if someone assisted her. Over and over again she lamented about getting old.

"Just you girls wait," she would say. "You're not far behind me and then you'll understand what I am facing."

And then in her wonderful jocular manner, she would occasionally add how much she would like to see that.

"I just wish I were around to see you go through what I am," she would say. "Then I could say 'I told you so' and then you'd understand."

A Helpless Feeling

It is heartbreaking to watch our loved one or the one we care for decline. How helpless we feel, but we need to remember the most important thing we can do is to be there so we can support and show love in every way we can. It is good to know that our loving Heavenly Father never takes His eyes off of His children, and we can trust them into His care.

Talking to God

Today I just want to say, "Thank You Father, for all You've done for me and for all Your goodness and mercy. I do not deserve anything, but You've given me so much. It's time to say how much I appreciate it. You are God Almighty – the Creator of all things, yet You are interested in me. I cannot even begin to understand You, but I do know that Your very character is Love. I want to say I love you with all of my heart. Amen.

Change in Plans

… Behold, to obey is better than sacrifice, …
1 Samuel 15:22b

I said it earlier. Getting old isn't for sissies. Right now, I am feeling helpless thinking about how I watched my once vibrant mother who had more energy than her three daughters combined, slowly fail. Mom had a zest for life, was a terrific cook, kept her house spotless, was super-organized, and loved to help others. Then slowly she was reduced to a shell of the woman we knew and loved, and it was hard to watch.

Because I was feeling quite a bit better and got over my health challenge (thank You Lord), I decided I was going to go along with David to the sports complex and would make a nice picnic lunch for us. I hadn't been there in ages and was pleased to hear that some of the girls in the office had asked about me. (Isn't that sweet?) I figured I'd see Mom after my walk and picnic lunch. But I was eager to spend time with David first and go to the sports complex.

However, after I'd made our lunch, a tired spell flooded over me, so I made myself a cup of tea, sat in my lazy-boy chair and read. I was hoping my energy would return, but it didn't. David took one look at my gray face.

"You don't have to come you know," David said in his most understanding way.

Reluctantly, I told him to at least take the lunch and share it with someone after hockey. David had an appointment with a customer after hockey anyway, so with me not going, it saved him from having to take me home first.

I sadly watched David drive away, and then felt I should call Mom. I wanted to tell her that Janet and I were planning on taking her out for breakfast tomorrow as long as I was feeling okay. I thought that would cheer her up.

I punched in her number. Immediately she answered.

"Oh Nancy, my memory is so bad, and not only that, I'm tired all the time."

"Mom, remember that you are 91 after all, so please do not be so hard on yourself."

She was quiet for a while.

"I feel like a dishrag," she said.

"Mom, you are a dishrag." I laughed.

"I'm an *old* dishrag!" was her quick answer.

We laughed and laughed. Soon we got talking about all the wonderful times we had in our childhood home. On and on the memories flooded over us and what one didn't think of, the other one did.

I remembered that our house was like Grand Central Station for all the relatives. I like to think that the reason we had so much company was because our home was happy, filled with love, and everyone felt good in that atmosphere.

I reminded Mom once again about breakfast the next day. She was thrilled and was eagerly looking forward to it. She did caution me that she might forget about it between now and then, but I assured her that the staff knew and would help her get ready. This gave her peace. So, even though I didn't get to go out with David, my morning turned out to be glorious. Just goes to prove that sometimes the alternative is even better than the original plan. It sure was today. I started to feel better.

Be Open to God for His Guidance

God sees our lives through different eyes than we do. He also has a better "view" than we do, for He sees our past, present, and future all in one, while we only see the past and this moment. We are very limited, but God is not limited by time or space, and therefore if we are in tune with Him, He can organize our days to be more than we'd ever imagine. Trust Him today to lead you, knowing His way is right.

Talking to God

Thank You God that Your ways are always best. Sometimes I can't seem to make sense of things that happen, but You know exactly what is coming. May I stay close to You so You can guide me. It is much easier to do things Your way, for then it is always right. Amen.

Shower Curtain

And whatever you do, do it heartily,
as to the Lord and not to men,
Colossians 3:23

I was trying to think of something different to do for an outing with Mom, when I came up with an idea. I would take her to visit our dear friend Lovada who was housebound due to a disability. Mom was thrilled. She had known Lovada even longer than I had, so I made the arrangements. We had a wonderful visit, but Mom soon tired, so we prepared to leave. Just before we did however, Mom said she had to go to the bathroom. I walked her there, closed the door and went back to visit with Lovada in the living room. Suddenly I heard Mom yell.

"Nancy, get in here right away!"

Lovada told me later that I had a look of horror on my face and went as white as a sheet. All kinds of scenarios played in my mind. Had she fallen and couldn't get up? Would I have to call 911? Did Mom have an accident on Lovada's beautiful rug?

"Oh Lord, please, not in Lovada's apartment!" I prayed. My legs barely carried me to the bathroom. I cautiously opened the door, not knowing what to expect. Much to my relief, Mom was smiling, standing by the tub.

"Nancy, have you ever seen a more beautiful shower curtain?" she said.

Relief flooded my entire body, almost to the point of weakness.

"Yes, Mom." I agreed that it was, indeed, a beautiful shower curtain.

Mom, totally unaware of the momentary panic that we had endured, thanked Lovada for a lovely time and toddled off down the hall toward the elevator.

Lovada and I never forgot that visit. Every time we got together, Lovada would say, "Oh Nancy, you should have seen your face." Then we broke into gales of laughter once more.

Mom would never find out about that day she filled me with fear in that moment. Oddly enough, however, I have to admit it was actually worth it simply because of the joy the memory still brings to this day.

Show and Tell

Do you have a funny story to tell about what either happened to you or to the one you care for? If it's not embarrassing or harmful, maybe you could share it. Most people need to hear a good story and have a good laugh, and this may be the exact "prescription" they need. Be sunshine to someone.

Talking to God

Father, You know how much good laughter does for me, for it was You who created laughter. May I become like a child and be able to laugh at myself over a situation as long as it doesn't hurt anyone. Thank You for laughter. Amen.

Fruit of His Labour

But seek first the kingdom of God and His righteousness, and all these things shall be added to you.
Matthew 6:33

David came with Janet and me to visit Mom and would be joining us for breakfast. Because Mom was convinced that it was David who had made her new teeth, he asked her a question. He wanted to make sure Mom had remembered to wear her dentures.

"Show me *my* teeth."

Mom proudly gave him a huge toothy smile. A while ago she had mentioned how she thought David would have been angry with her because she had forgotten to put her teeth in before supper one evening.

"And he worked so hard making them for me."

She was deadly serious. We tried to tell her that it wasn't David who made her new dentures, but Jason.

We finally stopped correcting her, and because it gave everyone a bit of a chuckle, we decided to have fun with it. I didn't realize I had such a talented husband who makes teeth and does such a great job!

Mom was happy to see us walk into her room and help her get ready for another restaurant breakfast. It didn't take long. Mom seemed keen. Janet, David, and I helped Mom out to the car.

Mom said, "I've been looking forward to this, and I do know for sure that we're going to "Joe's" for breakfast."

Janet questioned her, but Mom was adamant that we were on our way to Joe's. This made us laugh for there never had been a Joe's restaurant, that we knew of, in the Kitchener-Waterloo area. But she seemed certain there was. Instead of Joe's, we drove to our favourite restaurant and all was soon forgotten. We were thankful.

As we got seated the waitress greeted us. She remembered Janet, Mom, and me and then commented about how we brought an extra person. I introduced David. As she was pouring our coffee, Mom with a straight face asked, "Are my daughters behaving?"

The waitress chuckled and assured her that we were indeed behaving. Mom was satisfied. When the food came, Mom dug in.

"It tastes the same as last year," Mom said in between bites.

We looked at each other and laughed for it had only been a couple weeks since we were there. Mom was a happy little camper and ate "the best breakfast ever" while we chatted. All in all, it was a profitable day. David got to see the fruit of *his* work on Mom's teeth, and we enjoyed breakfast with her. Win-win.

Simple Things in Life

When it comes right down to it, it's often the simple things that mean the most. We do not have to undertake great feats, but if we take small steps that we know pleases those who are in our care, that often accomplishes more. Everyone is different, but it really takes very little to learn and eventually understand what works and what doesn't. The important thing is to pay attention and stay in tune with what is happening.

Talking to God

How I praise You God that Your resources are unlimited. If I ask You for ideas and help, You will never turn me away. You know my personality and what pleases me the most and can personalize my every move to be the best possible choices. Thank You for being intimately involved in my life. Amen.

Sad Mama

But when he saw that the wind was boisterous, he was afraid;
and beginning to sink he cried out, saying, "Lord, save me!"
Matthew 14:30

Mama is sad. We stopped in to see her after visiting friends after church that morning. When we arrived at Heritage House later that afternoon, we delivered a huge bag of my chocolate popcorn to the staff, along with a card, thanking them for taking such good care of our mother. I even had a goody bag for Mom. I knew something was wrong, though, because it was most unusual for her eyes not to light up when I showed her all the different chocolate treats I'd made. She didn't even want to try one. No interest at all. I'd never seen her turn down a treat like that, so I knew for sure she was experiencing some depression.

She was actually up and fully dressed when we walked in shortly after three o'clock, and when I realized she wasn't interested in the treats, I suggested we take some to Ken. She agreed, so we slowly walked down the hall. Many of the staff and some of the residents greeted Mom, but she showed no emotion whatsoever.

"Isn't it time that they take the Christmas decorations down?"

I had to smile and said, "Mom, it's only Dec. 16th and Christmas isn't until the 25th."

This obviously was news to her. When we made it to Ken's room, we saw he was in a deep sleep and didn't stir even though we were talking right beside his chair. We didn't want to wake him, so we left the treats and headed back down the hall. I thought we'd stop in the sunroom, but there was a family visiting in there. Guess they had the same idea. There were three boys playing a game and arguing over who had the most points. The mother was embarrassed.

"Don't worry, I had three brothers and we fought too, but we all turned out. Well, at least I did." David said.

The mother laughed. "So, there is hope?" We both assured her that there was, indeed, hope. I think she felt better. We walked back to Mom's room, but she kept talking about how small her world was and how she longed for Heaven. Once we were all sitting down, we sang "But Until Then[8]." Mom started to sob. My heart ached. It's tough growing old.

Call for Help

Sometimes when trials come, we simply need to call out, "Jesus help me," and He will. He is waiting for us to pray and ask for help and He is only too pleased to walk alongside us with love and compassion.

Talking to God

There are times when it's difficult to ask even You, God, for help. However, the truth is that often I simply cannot do it on my own. Thank You for helping me in any situation I find myself in. Thank you for giving me strength, wisdom, and grace to make it through. Amen.

[8] Lyrics by Carl Stuart Hamblen

When is Tomorrow?

Fear not, for I am with you; Be not dismayed, for I am your God. I will strengthen you, Yes, I will help you, I will uphold you with My righteous right hand.
Isaiah 41:10

How would you respond if someone asked, "When is tomorrow?"

When I called Mom before 8:00 a.m., I thought I had the wrong number, then realized it was her Personal Support Worker on the other end of the line. She inquired if I wanted to talk to Mom and then asked if we were taking her out for breakfast. I told the PSW that it wasn't this day, but the day after. She told me Mom wanted to speak to me.

"Oh Nancy, I am so confused. I don't know what to do next!"

I assured her that soon it would be time for her to go down for breakfast.

"Janet and I are taking you out for breakfast tomorrow," I said, hoping this would please her.

Besides, she liked to know ahead of time when we were taking her out. She told me that once, so I try to remember to do it. Mom paused for a moment.

"When is tomorrow?" she asked.

At first, I started to say, "After the next sleep, it will be tomorrow," but then had to backpedal because she naps right after breakfast and again right after lunch, so that didn't work. I tried to assure her that she did not need to worry her pretty little head about anything because the staff knew about our plans and Janet and I would be there to pick her up at the proper time. But even that didn't help. Poor Mama. Janet and I saw her slipping deeper and deeper into dementia and we felt powerless to stop it.

Our hearts were heavy, but we did know that Mom would be happy when we would arrive the next day to help get her coat on and take her to the car. Then she would dig into her breakfast and exclaim over and over, "This is the best breakfast I've ever had!"

When is tomorrow? *Tomorrow* would soon be here.

Our Lives Are Not Wasted

One never knows the gold we can find if we truly listen. I still have much to learn. Mom cannot even guess what her life is accomplishing even while suffering with dementia. She is still teaching me much. We may never know who our lives are touching by just being who God made us to be. Be encouraged!

Talking to God

You said in Your Word that You had a plan for my life even before I was born. You knew where I would be born, who my parents would be, and what my experiences would entail. Nothing is hidden from You. I truly want my life to count, so help me to make right decisions and to follow the path You choose. Amen.

Tomorrow is Today!

And whatever you do in word or deed,
do all in the name of the Lord Jesus,
giving thanks to God the Father through Him.
Colossians 3:17

Yesterday when I called Mom, she was quite confused, and I didn't know just how it would go today when Janet and I would take her out for breakfast. However, I was pleased to find Mom dressed nicely, sitting in her chair relaxing with her eyes closed. She was ready and waiting for Janet and me to take her out to breakfast. I gently touched her shoulder and received a huge smile when she saw me. She told me that she knew something was up when the nurse took such a long time getting her ready, but she didn't know what was going to happen. I knew right then that we were going to have a good morning.

Janet arrived and together we got Mom ready to go outside. I walked Mom to the door while Janet brought the car up. While we were in the hallway, Mom was unsteady on her feet even with me holding on to her and in a loud stage whisper said, "Pretend like we are like two drunk men." I laughed out loud and the nurse at the front desk laughed too.

"Well you didn't have to include me in the drunk men bit you know!"

We laughed again. Mom kept saying how much of a surprise this was the whole way to the restaurant. Then, when we arrived, Mom had difficulty getting out of the car. We were puzzled until we realized she still had her seat belt on.

"That'll do it every time!" I said. Another good chuckle.

"Do they still welcome us here?" Mom said as we walked into the restaurant. When we pointed out the welcome mat, it made her feel better. Janet and I got talking about Mom wanting to know when tomorrow was, and it was obvious Mom was listening.

"Well? When *is* tomorrow?" Without thinking I said, "Tomorrow is today!"

Even Mom laughed. She loved her breakfast and almost licked the plate clean. She kept thanking us for the wonderful holiday. I guess that's what it felt like to her.

When we tried to get Mom into the car, we had trouble. We did everything we knew to do, but for some reason she couldn't budge. Finally, we realized her hood was caught on the top of the door. No wonder we weren't getting anywhere. Just one of those days!

Mom loved being in the car, but we were always afraid that she'd get cramps and when that happened, we needed to move quickly! We decided to drive to the parking lot of Heritage House and just sit in the car chatting. Mom was happy with that and was thrilled with the heated seats.

We chatted about different things and finally Mom said, "Are we waiting for something?"

That was the icing on the cake. Janet and I roared with laughter. We took her back to her room and got her ready for a "nice nap," as she put it. I tucked her in, then leaned over to kiss her cheek, but the pendant I was wearing hit her in the face. Not quite the storybook ending like in the movies. Sometimes you just can't do *nothin'* right!

There are Good Times

Not all times are sad and gloomy, so, when the good times come, rejoice! Allow yourself to laugh out loud and enjoy the moment, even if it is just for a moment. There is always something to be thankful for, and it makes for a happy heart.

Talking to God

Father, thank You for the gift of laughter. How precious it is to simply forget my troubles and laugh. May I be able to see the lighter things in life and allow myself the freedom to let go. Amen.

When Trouble Comes

But You, O Lord, are a shield for me,
My glory and the One who lifts up my head.
Psalm 3:3

Mom was upset and so restless that she couldn't even nap (which was most unusual.) But she had good reason. Sometime in the morning, Ken fell and was taken by ambulance to the hospital. After an x-ray, they discovered his hip was broken. Mom broke her hip a year ago in June, so we understood all that went along with that diagnosis. Mom hardly remembered that ordeal, although Janet and I certainly did! Poor Mama felt terrible that she couldn't be with Ken. We assured her that his son, Jim and his wife Erma, were with him, but she still cried.

I saw her the morning of the fall before Ken's diagnosis of a fractured hip had been made. I wasn't sure if she remembered that he had fallen or not, so I just kept quiet. She seemed to know something had happened but didn't know what. We spent some time reminiscing and laughing over some funny things that happened to us over the years. Then it was Mom's turn.

"Ken fell and is in the hospital."

Her comment seemed so out of the blue. I gently told her that Ken had fallen, and the medical team would be taking x-rays to make sure nothing was broken. This seemed to soothe her, and she settled down. I left her to nap once I tucked her into bed.

When to Share Bad News

It can be difficult to decide when or even if we should share bad news to the one with dementia. Sometimes, it doesn't matter, but other times it does; so, where is that fine line? In this case, Mom remembered about Ken herself, so it took the decision out of our hands, but it isn't always that easy. Each situation is different, so tread carefully.

Talking to God

God, I am so confused sometimes as to what to share and what to withhold. How thankful I am that YOU know and can give me wisdom. I do pray for wisdom in these difficult situations and if I have to share, please give me the words that will help rather than hinder. Thank You. Amen.

Difficult Times

Blessed be the God and Father of our Lord Jesus Christ, the Father of mercies and God of all comfort,
2 Corinthians 1:3

After church we had a nice lunch with friends, and then stopped in to see Mom. She was in bed, but wide awake and couldn't stop talking about how Ken was in the hospital and how she couldn't be with him even though she wanted to be. I assured her again that his children were there, and he was not alone. But even then, she was restless and agitated. She got up, then laid back in bed, and then got up to sit in her chair but started to fall asleep, so I guided her back to bed.

I called Janet who said that although the doctors would do corrective surgery on Ken, they probably would not do a hip replacement, and he would be sent back to the home. That would make Mom more content. I thought about how frustrating it would have been for Ken to have a brain that wasn't working properly and then being in unfamiliar surroundings, unsure of what was going on.

Somehow, he knew that something awful happened, but there was nothing he could do about it. Our hearts ached for Ken, and for Mom who felt a similar helplessness.

Look Up!

There is something powerful about looking up. We tend to look down when we are hurt or discouraged, but God promises to "Lift up our Head" when we are in difficulty and we are to cry out to Him. Something wonderful can happen when we look up towards Heaven.

Talking to God

You are the great encourager. There is none like You and I stand in awe of Your power. Nothing can happen to me without

Your promise to be there to hold me when I, or my loved one, is hurting. How I praise You. Amen.

Christmas 2018

For unto us a Child is born, Unto us a Son is given; And the government will be upon His shoulder. And His name will be called Wonderful, Counsellor, Mighty God, Everlasting Father, Prince of Peace.
Isaiah 9:6

Christmas traditions are wonderful. Decades ago, the three of us girls and our husbands decided to set aside December 24th as the day we got together, and it's worked out very well. We call it, "Dubrick Christmas" and we have an absolute blast. We all congregate at someone's home and everyone brings finger food. We start eating immediately and graze all day.

Once we invited some friends, Ben and Jen, to join us, and as soon as they walked in the door, their food was whisked away. They barely had their coats hung up and they noticed other guests walking by with what they had brought, already on their plates. They thought it was a hoot! They fit right in.

Yesterday was the big day, December 24th. Soon family started arriving with great food and the feasting began. Hank and Janet brought Mom shortly after two-thirty, but she was fully expecting turkey, dressing, and gravy and was most disappointed to see only finger foods. I'd worked all morning preparing tasty morsels, but Mom felt cheated. We tried to explain that the Christmas meal was different for us from Thanksgiving, but I'm not sure she quite got it.

"I still don't understand why there isn't turkey, dressing, and gravy! Mom said.

"Mom, I'm sorry that you were expecting all of that. How disappointed you must be."

"Well, yes I am disappointed!" Mom grumbled.

Janet and I felt terrible, but the fact is that there was no turkey; only finger foods, just as it had been for decades. We were sad Mom forgot.

By four-thirty, Mom was more than ready to go home, but Hank and Janet didn't want to leave yet, so I put her on the couch in the den and she had a nice nap—which helped.

Mom was distressed about Ken, wondering how he was doing. She kept asking the same questions over and over. Janet and I would take turns patiently answering them. She somehow was feeling responsible for Ken's fall.

"If I wouldn't have been out partying, I could have helped him," she said.

We liked the "partying" part.

Once she said to me, "Oh Nancy, you have such a long drive home!"

I laughed and said, "Mom, we live in the upstairs apartment."

She laughed too when she got it. Finally, Hank and Janet took Mom home, but on her way out, Mom asked to see the hostess.

"Just be glad you don't have to look after me," she said to Tanya. Then she turned to our youngest granddaughters and thanked *them* for the good food.

"Just say 'You're welcome' to her," I whispered, which they hesitantly did.

"Oh Nana. You must be the most patient woman I know!" our 22-year-old granddaughter Samara said to me after Mom left.

She was right. It did take a lot of patience to answer the same questions over and over. And then one more time around the mountain for good measure. Mom didn't realize she was going though dementia, so we just loved her and tried to give simple answers. It didn't always help, but it was either that or ignore her, and we wouldn't have done that.

Look on the Bright Side

Sometimes special holidays didn't quite go the way we'd planned. Perhaps there were some disagreements, or dissention that clouded the event. However, we can often diffuse a potentially volatile situation with humour or simply change the subject. Or, if necessary, walk away. Our attitude is important. Do we contribute in a positive or negative manner?

We can often intervene with the prayer, "God, please come in our midst and change the atmosphere." And I know, from experience, that this works. With Jesus in our midst, He calms storms.

Talking to God

Christmas is often a time of love, family, joy, and peace, but it can also be a time of disharmony and chaos. Please show me how I can be a catalyst for peace, simply by remaining calm and calling out to You to intervene. You are the giver of peace, and I open up my heart to You. Amen.

Downhill

But those who wait on the Lord Shall renew their strength;
They shall mount up with wings like eagles,
They shall run and not be weary,
They shall walk and not faint.
Isaiah 40:31

Dementia is horrible. Mom was suffering more and more from the effects, it seemed. David and I stopped in to see her just before one o'clock on Boxing Day, when we were on our way to Matt and Sarah's. Mom was still in the dining room. She gave us a big smile when she saw us.

Then she said, in a loud whisper, "They are so slow here and I haven't even had my meal yet."

I did see a small dish of pudding, partially eaten in front of her. She repeated her complaint, a little louder this time. But this time one of the staff members heard her.

"Flo, you have eaten. This is your dessert."

I had to explain to Mom that she'd already eaten, but I could tell that she wasn't convinced. I then handed her some of my homemade goodies left over from Christmas and gave a few to her tablemates, too. They were delighted. After a short while, we walked back to Mom's room. She still couldn't believe she had eaten her noon meal, but I just let it go, for it didn't do any good to correct her.

I had called Mom the day before, to tell her I had found out that Ken would be released from the hospital that afternoon. I thought she'd be glad to hear the news. Instead, she wailed.

"Oh Nancy, you'll have to come right away because there's no way I can take care of Ken by myself."

"Mom, you don't have to take care of Ken. There is a doctor and nurses to look after him when he comes back."

"I don't know how to take care of him." Mom moaned, and no amount of assuring her would change her mind. A few days ago, she was worrying about him being in the hospital and longed to have him back at Heritage House, and now she was stressing about him returning.

I could see frustration and anxiety written all over Mom's face. She was carrying a load that was far too heavy, but she didn't know how to let it go. Sometimes you just can't win for losing. I assured her over and over that she did not have to look after Ken, but she could visit him whenever she wanted, but it didn't seem as if it was registering. It was getting a little frustrating, so I knew this was one of the times I just had to walk away.

"Well Mom," I said. "It's almost time for you to go to lunch. Why don't you take your cute little walker and head down there?"

Giving her something else to think about seemed to work. Mom's attitude changed and we said goodbye on a good note. What a relief. I called Janet to tell her all about the call and we both agreed how sad it was to see Mom's mind slipping and knowing that there was nothing anyone could do.

I prayed often for her and continued to visit and call as often as I could. Janet and I would try to take her out for breakfast which she loved. But somehow it just didn't seem enough. No matter how often we were there visiting or talking to her on the phone, we still felt guilty that we weren't doing enough. That made no sense because we still had other commitments that needed our attention. But it was our mother who was hurting, and we seemed powerless to do much to alleviate her pain.

When Things go Downhill

Some days it seems as if there is no light at the end of the tunnel, and it is tough. These are the times we must have the patience of Job and the wisdom of Solomon, portions of which are available when we ask. We may not always know exactly what to do, but God does, and He is there to give us what we need.

Talking to God

Lord, I am so needy. Some days hum along nicely, and then suddenly I may feel blindsided by what happens to the one I care about. Although there is only so much I can do, I ask that You bless those times greatly, so that I will be able to weather the storms when they come. Amen.

Two Moms

Seek the Lord and His strength; Seek His face evermore!
Psalm 105:4

One thing about dealing with a loved one with dementia, it's always an adventure!

Janet and I took turns visiting Mom. She and Hank went on Saturday, and David and I went on Sunday. We always phoned each other to get the 'lowdown' on how things went.

I felt sorry for Janet when she relayed how badly things were on Saturday. Apparently, when Mom saw Janet, she cried.

"I'm so glad you came before I die," she said in between sobs. "I just know I'm going to die, soon."

And it went downhill from there. Hank and Janet had taken Mom to see Ken, but that didn't go well either. Janet said that by the time they left she felt like a rung-out dishrag. So, when David and I walked into her room after church, we had no idea what we would face.

Mom was napping, so I gently touched her shoulder. She woke up with a smile and told us she'd just dozed off. Because she had her nightgown on, we suggested she stay in bed while we enjoyed a lovely visit. No drama, no tears, just a lot of memories of times past, and then we could see that she was tired, so we left. I couldn't wait to call Janet.

David jokingly said, "You should say, 'na-na-na-na-na. I got the good Mom and you got the difficult Mom this weekend!'" I laughed and said I should, but instead, I took pity on Janet and dropped it down a notch. I told her how good Mom was today and she laughed and said, "Well, lucky you!" I must say Janet is a good sport.

Good Times and Bad Times

Dementia is mean. It robs a person of reason and one wonders where our loved ones are. Sometimes we'd try to correct Mom, or reason with her, but that didn't always work. Changing the subject seemed to work the best, but there were times when even that didn't help. That was where love and patience did their best work.

Talking to God

It's difficult, Lord, to stay loving when the one I care for is unreasonable and irritable (and sometimes downright mean,) but I am aware that she does not want to be this way. Help me Father, for I cannot be loving on my own. Show me the best way to respond, for You know best. Amen.

Laughter Helps

A soft answer turns away wrath,
But a harsh word stirs up anger.
Proverbs 15:1

Today Janet and I walked into Mom's room at half past eight and she was dressed and sitting peacefully in her chair waiting. As we spoke to her, she told us that she had no idea just what she was waiting for, but she was ready, nonetheless, and thrilled to find out we were taking her out for breakfast. She'd forgotten that we had reminded her numerous times that we would be picking her up today to take her out.

As usual, at the restaurant, she kept saying how delicious breakfast was. After the plates were taken away, she commented how she had eaten a huge breakfast. We agreed.

"Was there any left over for you?" she asked.

Of course, we laughed and assured her we had our own plates, so that satisfied her.

Once we got Mom back to Heritage House, we were sitting in her room chatting with her.

"You can tell me something and I can't catch it," she said.

"You catch it, but you drop it right away," I quickly responded.

We all laughed.

"I've lost my marbles." Mom continued to despair about her failing faculties.

"There's a hole in your bucket," I said, smiling.

Then Janet joined in. "Dear Liza, Dear Liza."

We all roared with laughter again. It was good to laugh and let off a little frustration.

"Even if I forget most of it, I'm so glad you girls come as often as you do. It gets pretty lonely here, and your visits cheer me up, even though I don't always remember all that happens."

Precious words from Mom. She couldn't thank us enough for all we had done for her.

Good and Bad

We never know what state those in our care will be, so we must be prepared to accept the bad with the good. When they are in a good mood, rejoice and allow yourself to enjoy each moment. When things turn, simply accept it without judgement or anger, for it will probably pass. Enjoy the good and put up with the not-so-good. It will make things much easier on yourself and on them.

Talking to God

Father, I freely admit that I need You desperately. Without You, I will falter and do or say the wrong things at the wrong times and make things worse. Give me Your heart of love and compassion and show me how to freely model these qualities to others. Amen.

Interruptions

But as it is written: "Eye has not seen, nor ear heard, Nor have entered into the heart of man The things which God has prepared for those who love Him."
1 Corinthians 2:9

The phone rang around one o'clock in the afternoon, just as I put my feet up in my lazy-boy chair, intent on having a little nap. David answered the phone.

"Oh hi, Mom. Do you want to talk to Nancy?"

I'd pretty much figured it wouldn't be good, because Mom no longer had the mental capacity to dial the phone herself. I knew a PSW would only call us if Mom was over the top.

Unfortunately, I was right. Immediately Mom started in on how I had to come right away because her mind was bad and no one there could help.

"I didn't even know how to find my room," Mom said, her high-pitched tone revealing her anguish. "Ken won't talk to me, and I must have you come right now!"

I was silent for a while, as I thought through my approach.

"Mom," I eventually said, "You're right about your mind being bad, and we feel sad about it, but what could I do if I came?"

"Well I don't know, but they can't help me here!" she said.

"Did a nurse dial the phone for you, Mom?"

"Well you know that I can't do that." Mom seemed annoyed.

"Did a nurse help you back to your room after lunch?"

I think she caught on to my train of thought and begrudgingly said, "Well yes."

"Mom, they do help you there, and they care very much for you," I said.

This kind of took the wind out of her sails and I knew we'd just go around and around the same mountain if we kept this up. So, I changed the subject.

"Mom, I have to tell you about last night. We were invited to my cousin Paula's house for a New Year's Eve Party, and even Ron and Lois were there. We had a marvellous time."

She did brighten up when I mentioned her brother and his wife were there and told her what a great time we all had.

"And we didn't get home until 2:30 in the morning!"

"Wow!" Mom said. She was impressed with how late I stayed, because normally, I turn into a pumpkin around 10 o'clock at night.

However, she soon lost interest in what I was saying.

"What should I do now?" she wailed.

I reminded her about how she usually has a nap after her lunch, and that would be a good idea. A nurse then came on the line and thanked me for talking to Mom. She agreed that Mom needed a nap and she would help her settle down. Then, after she woke up, the nurse would give her a nice cup of tea and she'd feel better. And that was that. Mom was happy. And so was I!

How thankful I was for the staff that assisted and gently took care of their charges.

Thank a Staff Member Today

If your loved one or the one you are responsible for is in assisted living, it is important to stop and thank the staff for the job that they are doing. Unfortunately, it is easy to only speak to them if there is something wrong, and although it may be important to point that out, it shouldn't be the only time you speak to them. They are, after all, only human, and everyone makes mistakes. A smile, a small encouragement, a card, or a treat will go a long way to give encouragement to carry on with a job that comes with many challenges.

Talking to God

God, show me the importance of kindness. There is a saying, "Be kind; everyone you meet is fighting a hard battle."[9]

---

[9]Variant of the Christmas message "Be pitiful, for every man is fighting a hard battle," written by the Scottish preacher Ian Maclaren (also known as John Watson) in 1897.

Only You see just how difficult life is for that person at that moment, and perhaps they need someone to show understanding and love. May I be that person. Amen.

Compassion

See that no one renders evil for evil to anyone, but always pursue what is good both for yourselves and for all.
1 Thessalonians 5:15

I called Mom in the late afternoon. I figured she'd be up and around by then, and she was. I was pleased that she answered the phone. Sometimes I don't think she can figure out what to do when it rings so I was glad to see she managed well when I called. I realized, too late though, that I'd woken her up.

She launched into an angry tirade as to how she is sick of living, and this is a terrible place and on and on. I knew this was going nowhere, so I told her how difficult it was for Ken. She actually asked why it was difficult. She'd obviously forgotten about Ken's fall, so I reminded her (for the hundredth time) how he'd fallen and broken his hip. I told her again about how he was rushed to the hospital and eventually had surgery. I also told her that during his entire hospital stay he was agitated because he had no idea what was happening to him. Mom melted a bit with compassion. I could tell she actually felt sorry for someone other than herself.

"Well, how am I supposed to take care of him?" she asked. I once again explained that the doctors and nurses took excellent care of him, and Jim and Erma visited him often. I told her she could visit him, too, whenever she wanted to just hold his hand, because he liked that.

"And Mom, it's almost 5 o'clock, which means it's suppertime, and if you go now, perhaps you can talk to Ken for a bit. Wouldn't that be nice?"

Mom thought about what I had said and then agreed that that was exactly what she would do. I said goodbye and thankfully we hung up on a happy note.

How good it is that Mom can be easily distracted and therefore if she gets out of her funk, I'm glad. Now that I think of it, David does the same thing for me when I'm upset. Hmmm. Maybe I learned how to handle Mom from him!

During Troubled Times

We all need encouragement. Sometimes we feel as if we are not making a difference as we plod along day after day, but that is not true. Every kindness is noted in Heaven. Every sacrifice does not go unnoticed. It's the little things that can cause someone to either carry on or give up. Many times, those we encourage turn around and encourage us. When we give, it somehow comes back to us. When we love, love comes back in ways that we would never guess. Never give up doing the right thing.

Talking to God

I am often so weak, Father, and feel as if I am not doing enough or it isn't counting. You promised that Your eye is on the sparrow, and that not one falls without You noticing. What I do does count, and I ask that You help me to remember that the next time I get discouraged. Amen.

Trouble in Paradise

Keep me as the apple of Your eye;
Hide me under the shadow of Your wings, …
Psalm 17:8

"I've got to stop giving in to the demands that everyone is putting on me!"

These were the words Mom spoke right after she heard me on the phone. Of course, I wasn't sure what she was talking about, but I listened for a while and then asked her a question.

"What demands do people put on you Mom?" My poor Mama couldn't come up with anything.

Then she shifted her thoughts and talked about how her eyes were bad and she just couldn't keep up. Mom was constantly concerned that she was losing her sight, but the next minute she would point out a small bird in the bush outside her window. In the winter she might notice gentle snowflakes.

One time when Hank and Janet were there, she lamented to them about her poor eyesight. Then she suddenly noticed some activity happening outside her window.

"Mom, can you see that truck in the parking lot?" Hank asked.

"Yes, I can see it, but I can't see the man standing next to it!" Mom said.

Hank and Janet had a hard time to keep from laughing because she was dead serious about not being able to see the man.

We tried to convince Mom that her eyes were fine, but I know it was her mind that had trouble interpreting what she saw. Some days she'd agree with us that this was true. But in the next breath, she would complain again that her eyes were bad. Oh dear. Poor Mom.

A bit later in our phone conversation, she told me a concern she had about her clothes. "Every once in a while, I find myself wearing someone else's clothes and they don't fit me properly."

"Mom, I always look in your closet whenever I'm there and have never seen anything that doesn't belong to you, so you don't need to worry about that."

I tried to keep my voice low and assuring.

"Well, if they're mine, why don't they fit sometimes?"

I mentioned that our body changes shape from time to time. Sometimes we gain weight and sometimes we lose weight, but it's all good. She seemed fine with that explanation.

Soon it was time for her to go to lunch, but before she hung up, she gave her last bit of direction for the day.

"Make sure and use my phone more, okay?"

Sure Mom, I will use your phone more, and I'll try to call a bit more often too!

When Overwhelmed

I have found that whenever I am overwhelmed, I speak the Name of Jesus. Very soon, the anxiety, depression, and worry leaves, and I am at peace. King David found this to be very helpful, as he often found himself asking God to cover him with His wings. Try it next time you feel overwhelmed and see what happens. If it helped King David, perhaps it will help us also. Worth a try.

Talking to God

Father. There are times when I feel as if I will be overcome with all the difficulties of life. Waves of anxiety or grief wash over me, and other times, I feel as if I am in a dry and barren desert. Either way, how thankful I am that You promised to be with me. You long to comfort me if I am willing to be still. Thank You for Your love and compassion. Amen.

God's Idea

I will instruct you and teach you in the way you should go; I will guide you with My eye.
Psalm 32:8

P*ick up some lunch for your Mom today.* The thought that came into my mind during the sermon at church played out a few times. My mind wasn't wandering because the sermon was dull. Not at all. It was most interesting, actually, but I knew this thought came from the Lord. And I also knew that God spoke whenever He wanted to—probably thought now was a good time because I was silent!

So that's what we did. (Pastor Chris, if you're reading this, please note that I *was* listening to your excellent sermon on Discipleship. I really was!)

After the service, David quickly called Heritage House to keep Mom from eating lunch before we arrived. When we got there, we found her sitting in the hallway looking forlorn. Apparently, she'd had a meltdown.

A nurse came over and said, "This is perfect timing. Thanks for doing this for your Mom as she's had a bad morning."

We all went down to the sunroom and laid hamburgers, fries, and the all-important ice cream treat out on napkins. Mom was thrilled.

"Well I never expected anything like this to happen," she kept saying, over and over.

After we had settled down to eat, Mom cleared her throat and proudly made an announcement directly to David.

"David, I'm safekeeping the teeth you made for me."

But we noticed she didn't have them in, so I hurried down to her room to get them. Mom still truly believed that David made her teeth for her. We just went along with it, because most times it didn't matter. Besides, we thought it was cute.

After I helped Mom pop her dentures in, she enjoyed some of her hamburger and moved on to the fries with plenty of ketchup.

"This ketchup likes me!" she said, pointing to the ketchup with one of her fries.

Then she announced she was thirsty and requested some water. I hurried once again to her room and brought her water back. My food was getting cold, but it was for a good cause, and besides, I was burning calories going back and forth. Win-win!

Once Mom spotted the ice cream treat, she asked for "just a spoonful," but as soon as she tasted it, the hamburger and fries (with ketchup that likes her) were forgotten. I gave her some tea at the end and she happily slurped it until a couple minutes later.

"Where did that tea come from?" she asked.

We laughed.

"Nancy, I remember that you worked in the church library, so I knew that's where you were earlier!"

It was true that I did volunteer in the library after the service at our church but hadn't mentioned it in years. Funny how Mom's mind worked. She couldn't remember where the tea suddenly appeared from, but she recalled that I was a librarian on Sundays. Interesting!

And Mom remembered hymns. As Mom mentioned one after we'd finished eating, I'd start singing it. Then David and Mom joined in. Mom's lovely voice had faltered, but we were thrilled that she still tried and was able to recall the lyrics. After our lovely hymn-sing, we got talking about Heaven.

Mom kept repeating, "We will have all eternity to talk about things. And that's the last of my sermon."

I laughed and said, "Thanks Mom, but we already heard a sermon today."

We laughed again. All in all, it turned out to be a very good lunch time with Mom and something she desperately needed. I may not have known how bad a morning she'd had at the time, but God did, and when He whispered it in my ear during the sermon, I was very glad I had listened and obeyed.

Listening to Direction

It is so comforting to know that even when we don't know what we should do, God does. He knows best because He can be everywhere at the same time. He saw how much my Mama needed to have an indoor picnic to lift her spirits, and in turn, it lifted mine. Listen carefully to the nudges, for they could very easily be from the Holy Spirit.

Talking to God

How exciting to know that You are aware of every person on our planet. That's over 7 billion people, yet, You are able to know me intimately. How precious Your thoughts are, and how beautiful it is when I hear the gentle guidance to do something for others. If I listen, I will hear Your voice and it will be perfect timing with amazing results. Amen.

Indoor Picnic

Now may the Lord of peace Himself give you peace always in every way. The Lord be with you all.
2 Thessalonians 3:16

"Oh Nancy, September is a special month and I feel so alone."

This was the greeting when I walked into Mom's room just before noon hour. It took me a bit to understand, but I realized that both Mom and Ken celebrated birthdays in September, plus their wedding anniversary, so she must have been thinking about those. But it wasn't September. Snow was on the ground. But Mom hadn't made the connection.

I suggested we sit on the couch because I had a treat for her. Mom was keen but just before I opened the cooler bag, a staff member came in with Mom's laundry. She apologized for intruding, but I told her that it was okay and that we are about to have a picnic.

"Inside I hope!" she said.

I laughed and said, "Yea, it's kind of chilly out there."

Mom's eyes got big when I took out summer sausage, soft rolls, butter, and homemade pickled beets out of my cooler. It was good to listen to her "ooh" and "aah" her way through the entire meal.

"Does David still like the teeth he made?" Mom asked in between bites.

I laughed and pointed at her mouth.

"I don't know, 'cause they are in your mouth!"

Mom just smiled. As she ate, she also lapsed into a bit of mourning about the loss of her eyesight Then, a few seconds later, she looked toward the window.

"Oh look, it's snowing outside. Aren't the flakes tiny?"

I had to agree, and we carried on. I noticed she had her eyes closed as she chewed. It was like she had discovered that she could taste better when she had her eyes closed. I thought I would have a go, so I closed my eyes, too. By gum, she was right!

For dessert, I'd picked up a large fresh apple fritter donut from the Deli. It thrilled her to no end to sink her teeth into that. I cut little chunks off at a time, but she kept asking for more. At one point she mused that a nice cup of coffee would help, so I told her to wait until I got her a cup. When I came back into the room she smiled and said, "I cheated." Sure enough, that chunk that I had just broken off, was gone. The stinker. We laughed and laughed.

"My girls are spoiled," She said in between savouring more of the fritter. I just smiled. When she'd finally had enough, we just sat and talked. After a while she spotted the remaining half of the apple fritter on her TV tray.

"What is that?"

"An apple fritter."

"Did I have any?"

I laughed and said, "Yea, lots."

But then she asked for more and it was if she was tasting it for the first time. She then told me to take the rest home to David, so I packed it away.

Before I left, I called Janet (who'd been sick) to let her talk to Mom. They had a nice chat about our picnic lunch, then Mom was ready for a nap. I tucked her in and felt like I was putting my baby to bed. I think she was asleep before I left the room.

When I arrived home, Nathan was there and helped me with some computer stuff. Then it was time for lunch. As we ate together, I told Nathan about the funny things Mom had said. Then I opened the bag that held the last of the apple fritter. I asked Nathan if he'd like some.

"What is that?" he said. Without thinking I blurted out, "An apple fritter." Then I realized he'd copied Mom's reaction. We burst out laughing and then I playfully smacked him (smart aleck)!

All in all, it had been a lovely day for an indoor picnic. And I'm so glad Mom and I enjoyed it together. Oh, and yes, I did give David the rest of the apple fritter, once Nathan had had a taste (what fun!)

Something Different

Even if the weather is cold and miserable, it doesn't have to be gloomy inside. A small thing like an indoor picnic can brighten up any day. Just make sure to include an oversize apple fritter!

Talking to God

Oh Lord, how wonderful that I can enjoy the little things in life and, in the process, make memories that will last. These things give me great pleasure at the time, and in the future, I can open up the memory box at any time and recall them with a smile. Amen.

Difficult Phone Call

... Everywhere and in all things I have learned both to be full and to be hungry, both to abound and to suffer need.
Philippians 4:12b

"Will you be that patient with me someday?" David asked me that question after I hung up from a long, difficult conversation with Mom. We'd been helping in the kitchen at our seniors' luncheon for four hours, and I was beat. I'd been washing tons of dishes and being on my feet the whole time was tiring. When we got home, David began working on the computer. He was on a deadline for a project. I read for a while and then pushed my recliner back for a nice little nap. I needed that. When I woke up close to five o'clock, I decided to phone Mom.

"Hi Mom,"

"Oh Nancy, you woke me up."

"Oh sorry, but it's time to get up and go for supper now."

"What do you mean, supper? I have my nightgown on and am ready to go to sleep for the night."

"It's not bedtime yet, Mom. Can you see that it's still light outside?"

"Well, yes, but I'm comfortable and I want to go back to sleep."

This went on and on for quite a while. It felt like I was just spinning my wheels. I changed the subject. Always a good plan. I mentioned the delicious chili that my cousin, Murray, and his wife, Sharon, made and how hard we worked cleaning up at the Achievers' luncheon at church earlier in the day. Mom thought that was nice and remembered how she and Ken went to many of those luncheons over the years. It was a pleasant memory for her. We chatted about our indoor picnic the day before and, thankfully, she remembered that well.

I tried once more to tell her that she should get up, put some clothes on and go for supper, but it was too confusing for her. I understood. So I let it go and told her to relax for a few more minutes. I knew someone would be in to help her get up and take her down to the dining room.

It must be horrible to be that confused. Although I laugh about some of our antics together, my heart breaks for her. We are all very thankful for the excellent staff at Heritage House who take good care of our mother. After supper Mom will be more than glad to go to bed for the night. There's always a ribbon of light in every dark situation, and we thank God for that.

Confusion Is Tough

I'm sure each one of us has had moments of confusion ourselves, but in dementia or Alzheimer patients, it is multiplied many times over. How awful that must be for them. Rather than trying to clear things up, we should either change the subject, or simply allow things to happen as they will. It is a good thing for those for whom we care and takes the pressure off of us.

Talking to God

Dear God. Sometimes I feel so frustrated and wonder if I'm making any headway. You see these times and You, more than anyone, totally understand, for You see me as I am, and love me regardless. Give me an extra dose of peace, patience, kindness, and love in the difficult moments I pray. Amen.

Dementia Fog

And let us consider one another in order to
stir up love and good works, …
Hebrews 10:24

David and I were pleased to see how calm and peaceful Mom was when we visited Sunday afternoon. We had brought along her favourite ice cream treat. She'd loved every spoonful as we sat in front of her window with the sun's rays pouring through. We enjoyed sweet fellowship for a while.

Finally, Mom was getting tired. After she nodded off for a nap, we slipped out and came home to rest. I put my feet up and called Janet to recap all the things that had gone well with Mom. What we didn't know, was that dementia would slip in, and our mother would be beside herself once again.

One of the staff members called Janet later that evening. Mom was upset and demanded that Janet and I come right away.

"There are a lot of wrong things going on here and I need you!" Mom had told Janet. In a calm voice, Janet asked her about the wrong things.

"I can't even say because there's so much," Mom said.

We'd heard this kind of conversation many times before, so Janet quietly assured her that although neither of us would come, she could talk as long as she wanted. Gradually, Mom calmed down. Janet had suggested she find a staff member and ask them for a cup of tea. Janet told her then she could go to sleep. This suggestion sat well with Mom and she agreed to do just that.

Janet and I remember all too well receiving calls from the staff at the retirement home when Mom lived there; her home at St. Jacobs Place. There were no locks on the doors, so when Mom would threaten to run away, we had to get there as quickly as possible. We had no idea why she would want to escape from a five-star retirement home, and probably she didn't either, but we had no choice but to go and help out.

I'll never forget the first time Mom threatened to run away from the nursing home where there was a controlled entrance. Relief flooded us because we knew that she would be safe. When she threatened to leave at times, we just listened to her.

"Make sure to take an umbrella, because it's raining." "Be sure to dress warm," if it was cold, we would tell her. Of course, that wasn't what Mom wanted to hear, but when we'd call the staff later, we'd find out that she was feeling better. The crisis always passed.

Both Janet and I assured the staff that when Mom was in one of her dementia fogs, they could call either one of us and we'd gladly talk her down. Sometimes she just needed to hear one of our voices to be assured she wasn't alone.

Not Alone

We all need to know that someone cares, don't we? At times, life can be scary, and we want reassurance that we can go to someone who truly loves us and cares enough to soothe our worries. How thankful I am that we have Jesus as that Someone, no matter what time of day or night. He is always there and has promised never to leave us or forsake us. What peace that brings.

Talking to God

Heavenly Father You have promised that You would never leave me or forsake me. Sometimes I forget that You are always by my side, and never take Your eyes off me for a second. This is mind boggling, because I can only be in one place at a time, but You don't have those boundaries. Thank You for never leaving me alone–even for one second. Amen.

A Close Call

But the fruit of the Spirit is love, joy, peace, longsuffering, kindness, goodness, faithfulness, gentleness, self-control. Against such there is no law.
Galatians 5:22-23

Mom was dressed nicely and was lying on the bed when I arrived. The staff had helped her get ready, assuring her I would be there shortly. They hadn't taken her to the dining room for breakfast as they usually did at 8:00 a.m. because they knew we were taking her out. Yet Mom was thrilled and seemed a little shocked to see me.

"Oh Nancy, this is so good. What a surprise!" she repeated over and over.

When Janet arrived, she exclaimed again at how pleased she was with this surprise, and gleefully allowed us to get her ready to go out the door. I think this "surprise" thrilled her more than if she would have remembered about our breakfast date.

Before Janet arrived, I saw that Mom didn't have her dentures in or her glasses on, so I helped her with both. When I handed her her dentures, I guess I handed them to her upside down. She was having trouble figuring how to get them in.

"Oops mom," I said, when I saw the problem. "I must have handed them to you the wrong way."

She accepted my apology and laughed.

"You know, I have enough trouble on my own without you adding to it!"

I had to laugh and totally agreed with her. As we walked out of the home, Mom said, "I don't know what I did to deserve such royal treatment, but I am so very thankful."

One thing about Mom is that she shows appreciation for everything we do, unless she's deep in dementia—then nothing is right.

As we ate our breakfast, Janet and I were amazed at how much food that thin woman ingested, but it warmed our hearts to see her enjoying herself so much.

We'd paid the bill and were finishing our coffee, when mom said, "I really think we should be on our way, because I need to be in my own bathroom."

Those words are scary to us because of some past "accidents." We made sure she was able to make it back, not wasting a minute, hurrying Mom out the door and into the car. Janet put the pedal to the metal, and we made it back, just in time. Whew! Thank You God for all different kinds of blessings.

Be Vigilant

It is important that we are in tune with our charge, and to be aware of any reasons for concern. Once we are aware of any trouble, we can step in and help out. Accidents happen. We need to reassure and then help in any way we can. It's called unconditional love.

Talking to God

There are times when all I want to say is, "Thank You." Thank You for all the love, compassion, and patience you show me every day. May I learn to give to others what You have freely given to me. Amen.

Everyone Has a Story

Those who are wise shall shine Like the brightness of the firmament, And those who turn many to righteousness Like the stars forever and ever.
Daniel 12:3

We are all products of our upbringing. Early on, we send out feelers to know how to act. We quickly learn what behaviour is acceptable and what is not; what we can get away with and what we can't. We learn habits and social skills from our parents and watch carefully how they react in all situations.

Janet, Jane, and I always wondered why our mother was so shy and did not like any attention from strangers. She was only comfortable around family members, and then lo-and-behold she gave birth to three girls with outgoing personalities. Go figure!

When we were older, Mom shared how she had said, "please" and "thank you" to her fraternal grandmother once and was shot down.

"Stop it. We don't act all uppity around here!" she had said.

To her grandmother, this was almost a sin, so Mom learned to not say that again and to remain quiet.

Janet, Mom, and I discussed that hurtful reprimand the last time we went out for breakfast. Janet told us how, many years ago, one of her Sunday School teachers had taught her how important it was to say "please" and "thank you," even at home. That had been a shock to Janet at the time, but she remembered it and from then on, did just that. It was one of those moments she would never forget. I was intrigued by Janet's story. I had not realized that we didn't say please or thank you very often in our home, but perhaps after what Janet learned, we did it more often.

Our mother had low self-esteem. She rarely got involved in anything other than being with family, church, making our singing dresses, and going with us to singing engagements. Ten years after daddy died, she married Ken and together they both kept to themselves a lot, except for family and were happy with that arrangement. However, now that they were both in long term care and struggling with dementia, Mom felt as if she had no one to talk to when we weren't there. We tried to encourage her to join in with the many activities offered by the home, but she refused. The key could well be her childhood and how she felt inferior to all the other children. As a result, she learned to keep to herself. Our hearts ached for her, but there was really nothing we could do about something that was so ingrained in her life.

Do Not Judge

God only knows the real person inside each one of us and why we act the way we do. He sees the hurts, wounds, and memories deep inside our hearts and understands us completely. This is why He alone is the Judge, for He knows our past, present, and future.

I, for one, am far too quick to judge and have no right doing so, for I have not walked in another's shoes.

Talking to God

Oh God, remind me that hurting people often lash out, or are loud and obnoxious because they want to be noticed. Even bad attention is still attention to some poor souls. Or, as in Mom's case, they withdraw and seem almost haughty, but really inside, they are dying. Help me to keep trying to show love, for many desperately need someone to give a hug, a smile, or just good attention without judging, which could possibly make a difference. Help me to be that someone. Amen.

Excellent Advice

… I have come that they may have life,
and that they may have it more abundantly.
John 10:10b

Mom gave me two pieces of wise advice today. On our way to see her, David and I had stopped to buy her some tiny chocolate bars that she likes, from the dollar store. Sometimes she fancied something sweet. Everyone likes a treat now and again. When we got to Mom's room, she wasn't there. We went to Ken's room down the hall, and there she was sitting in his wheelchair watching Ken in his bed. He was fast asleep. I gently touched Mom's shoulder and she started to cry.

"Oh Nancy, it's so good to see your face. You have no idea how horrible it is for me here and Ken is going through so much that he can't respond but does nothing but sleep all the time."

My heart ached and I rubbed her back.

"I know that it's hard Mom, and I feel so bad for you," I said in a low voice.

She finally settled down and seemed deep in thought. Ken never woke up all the time Mom was there. I finally asked her if she'd like if we went back to her room. I reminded her that the sun was streaming in her window and we had brought her some sweets. She readily agreed it was time to return to her room. When we got there, I opened the drawer where I'd put the chocolate. Her eyes twinkled with glee when she saw it. We sat on the bed.

"You know Nancy, when I can't remember something, or my mind is really bad, you know what I say?"

I admitted that I didn't know, so she enlightened me.

"I say two things, "Who cares?" and "I don't give a hoot!"

I laughed and she repeated it. David and I rewarded her with more laughter each time and her mood changed in front of my eyes. After our giggling subsided, I tucked her into bed for her nap and she thanked us profusely for coming. We quietly left.

So, there you have it, dear friends. When life gets you down, or you don't know what to do or even which end is up, say these magic, insightful words: "Who cares?" and, "I don't give a hoot!" It worked for Mom and I'm sure it will work for you.

Seven Words to Help When Frustrated

We can learn a lot from Mom's advice. Maybe they could save us from a lot of stress. "Who cares?" and "I don't give a hoot!" These seven words could keep us all from being overwhelmed. It's so cute that you'll just have to laugh, and that will be half the battle.

Talking to God

Lord, sometimes I carry too many burdens that aren't mine. I care too much what other people will think, when in reality, it is Your opinion of me that should be the most important. May I understand when to help others and when to ask for help from others. When to care about others' needs and when to leave it with You. Amen.

To Give or Not to Give

… 'Not by might nor by power, but by My Spirit,'
Says the Lord of hosts.
Zechariah 4:6b

Sometimes it's difficult to be on the receiving end. I was raised in a home that stressed giving. Our motto was, "It is more blessed to give than to receive," and Mom gave us many examples of how to give with great joy. Of course, that is a very good trait to have, but when it came time to be on the other side, I couldn't handle it at first. I'm not sure if it was pride or just the fact that I didn't feel worthy to receive, but I struggled deeply when I could no longer give, and had to receive kindness and help from others.

In 1992, my body shut down and I was in bed 22 out of 24 hours a day. I thought I was dying. I had even planned my funeral for I figured it must have been serious. Turned out that I was suffering from Chronic Fatigue Syndrome (CFS) and it would continue for many years.

Church ladies set up a schedule to have meals prepared for my family, each Sunday for weeks, David would often find packages in the church freezer with our name on it. Whenever we sat down to those lovingly prepared meals, I would cry, and my husband and sons couldn't understand why. I was crying out of gratitude for I knew the meals were made with love. It was a humbling experience.

I recalled Hank's mother saying once in her heavy German accent, "If you don't receive, then you rob someone of a blessing."

I'd never thought of it quite that way before. If no one received, then 'givers', wouldn't be able to give.

As I cared for Mom, I recalled how often she helped others without anyone else knowing. Everything she did was in the background, and she liked it that way. She may not have been able to help others anymore, but still, her legacy would carry on in our hearts. I often wondered if she understood that she was now on the receiving end, and if that bothered her, since she was such a giver.

I would rather have been on the giving end of things, too, but sometimes, I had to receive with a thankful heart, and then, when things turned around, I would do my best to find a way to pay it forward. One way I learned to do that was to help Mom to the best of my ability. Another way was to give encouragement cards. I'd always been drawn to box sets of cards and kept a hefty pile of them in my cupboard. I found it a challenge to match the perfect card for the person I was reaching out to and I was always delighted when it happened. Because I loved to write, I usually bought blank cards with a nice picture and verse on the cover, which left lots of room for my ramblings. It was a good way to extend my caregiving *and* to pay it forward.

To Give or Receive? That is the Question

It doesn't really take a lot of time or effort to send a card to someone you know who is a caregiver or to the one you are caring for. We all need to be encouraged, and cards are something that can be looked at often.

For those of you who can't think of things to say, I suggest buying cards that have lovely verses in them and then add a Bible verse or a quote you've been impressed with, or just a note saying that they are in your thoughts and prayers. A little will go a long way.

We can all be givers, and enjoy the warm fuzzies it brings, and then when it's our turn to receive, we can do it with a thankful heart and accept it with the spirit it is given and allow others the joy of giving.

There is something very special that happens when we reach out and give to others, and sometimes that special feeling is even greater when we give in secret. However, there are also times when we can receive what others give to us with graciousness. The balance works well and either way, someone is blessed.

Talking to God

Dear God. How I thank You for all the gifts that You have bestowed upon me. You taught me how to give joyfully and how to also accept from others with a thankful heart. Both are designed by You and I can appreciate both in their proper seasons. Show me how to give and how to receive. Amen.

Laughing is Good

Rejoice in the Lord always. Again I will say, rejoice!
Philippians 4:4

I was sitting in my chair in a pool of sunshine, enjoying myself when Mom called.

"Oh Nancy, you and Janet have to come because I can't take it anymore!"

My poor mother was crying, and I felt awful.

I gently asked her what was wrong.

"I just left Ken sitting alone," she wailed, "because I couldn't do it any longer. It's not because we don't get along, because we do, but it was just too much!"

I assured her that we knew that she and Ken got along well and reminded her that she did not have to sit with Ken and watch him sleep. She was silent for a few seconds.

"Well, he does sleep a lot."

"Mom, do you want to know how you made a lot of my friends happy?"

She was curious, so I reminded her about the last time David and I visited and how she gave those two wonderful pieces of advice: "Who cares!" and "I don't give a hoot!"

I laughed at this and soon Mom was laughing too. We both said it over and over. I shared what my friends had said about how they were going to use that advice themselves when things went wrong. She loved it. We agreed that she should be taking her own advice and just like that, she said that she would. Then, she told me that it was stuffy in her room, and that she was dressed too warm.

"Whenever I'm too hot, I'm miserable," I told her, hoping she would make the connection.

I then told her to ask a staff member to help her put on something lighter. She assured me she would.

At Heritage House, there is a large meeting room at the end of the hall. Sometimes Mom called it "the chapel," or "the library," or "the assembly room" but we always knew what she meant. That time she called it "the celery room" (instead of assembly room). Mom realized her slip up and we laughed and laughed again.

Making others laugh is a high priority in our family. Then she said, "I don't think I'll go down for lunch (it was 11:50 a.m.) but I'll just have them bring me up a tray."

"But Mom, that's more work for them, and I don't think that's nice."

"I don't give a hoot!" she said.

Oh, but how we roared. We ended the call on a light note that day and both of us felt much better.

Lighten Up

We used to have an elderly Pastor who said, "If you don't laugh, you'll cry." and we found that to be true. Sometimes it may be difficult to find any laughter, but if you look hard enough, it will be there, and it will lighten the load you are carrying.

Talking to God

I know, Father, that it is better to have a happy heart than a heavy one. Please show me how to do that in every situation. Give me joy that can only come from You. Amen.

Wishful Thinking

Commit your works to the Lord,
And your thoughts will be established.
Proverbs 16:3

I love when I have a nice dream, because it is so, well ... nice! How wonderful to still be in that good dream just before coming to consciousness, and then lying there reveling in the happiness it brings. However, when it's a bad dream, I often wake up in a panic and it takes a while for me to realize that it is only a dream and I am safe in my home, and in bed beside my husband.

When Janet visited Mom the other day, Mom told her about a nice dream she had had. In her dream, she and Ken were moving back into the condo in the city. Apparently, she had sighed and told Janet how she wished it was true.

Mom and Ken did have a good life for 25 years when they lived in their cute condo in Kitchener. Ken was retired, and they were foot-loose and fancy-free, eating out a lot, going for long walks, or putting their fold-up bikes in the car and driving to Niagara Falls. There they would find a room, and travel along all the beautiful paved paths. In summers, they would park their trailer either at Mom's brother's property near Owen Sound, or at her sister's property so they could relax and enjoy the great outdoors. For many winters, they'd happily go to Florida. There they would buy bikes to use and then sell them before they left to come back home.

Their life was one big happy dream; until it became apparent that they could no longer take care of themselves. Slowly, their lives changed. At first, they moved into a beautiful five-star retirement home, but after a couple of years, Ken's dementia worsened and eventually he had to be moved to long-term care. Mom was alone until a year later, when she fell and broke her hip. The rest is history. Post-surgery, the anesthetic accelerated the dementia that Mom was already experiencing and before we knew it, we were moving her to long-term care, too.

"If only I could take a brush and white-wash these last few years, I would be happy," Mom lamented one day during her transition.

Our hearts ached for her, for so much had been ripped away. Ken and Mom still loved each other, but Ken often didn't seem to know her, which broke Mom's heart. When he did remember, they would sit and hold hands, sometimes singing their favourite hymns. But those times became few and far between. I hoped that Mom could enjoy more of those lovely dreams until the day God took her to her Heavenly home. I often wished my dear heart mother, sweet dreams while she was still with me.

Remembering

We often look at our own past through rose-coloured glasses. Thankfully, we can usually forget the bad and only remember the good and then we sometimes long for bygone years. It is important to listen to those we are caring for to hear their stories, for it also helps them to escape their daily realities, even if it's for just a short time.

Talking to God

Dear Lord, we humans have a great ability to remember our past, and when we recall the good times, it makes us feel nostalgic, but also, happy. Help me to know when "going down memory lane" is a good thing and when it simply drags me down. May I live in the present more and more and be thankful for all You have given us. Amen.

Worried Mother

Cast your burden on the Lord, And He shall sustain you; He shall never permit the righteous to be moved.
Psalm 55:22

"Oh Nancy, I thought you and David must have been in a car accident."

These were the words that Mom greeted us with when we visited her after church.

"I'm so relieved to see that you are okay."

We were puzzled as to what she was talking about because we didn't tell Mom we were coming. In fact, because it was so stormy, we weren't at all sure if we'd even get out of our driveway.

Our home is in the country, and sometimes the roads aren't as well plowed on weekends, but we thought we'd try it and turn around if it was going to be too much, but it turned out to be fine.

I always walk into Mom's room first because I never know Mom's state of dress or undress. This time she was facing away from the door.

I cheerfully said, "Hi Mom!" when I walked into her room.

Instead of turning around, she made her way over to the window, and the more I said hello, the more she pressed closer to the window. Finally, I reached out and touched her. She jumped and that's when she started asking about us being in a car accident. I made her sit on the couch with me and I told her she could calm down because we were there in one piece and had not been in a car accident. It took a while for her to settle, but she eventually did.

Then just like that she noticed a bottle of hand cream on the windowsill.

"I do remember Janet saying that I should put this lotion on my dry skin."

I agreed and immediately put some on her arms and face. Then, I noticed her dry heels, so I pulled her pant legs up, knelt down, and began to massage some of the fragrant lotion onto her legs and feet. She enjoyed every second. As I continued to massage the lotion in, we got talking about Jesus washing the disciple's feet. At one point, as we shared this intimate moment it almost felt like I was on Holy ground.

When we finally arrived home, there was a message on the machine. Apparently, Mom had called before we visited. She must have been in an angry mood.

"Come on ... come on.!"

I could tell she wasn't happy.

"Why aren't you talking?" she continued. "You know it's me and that's why you won't answer. Well, you'll find me walking downtown somewhere!"

Mom hadn't realized it was just the answering machine that had responded. She likely thought that I had answered but wouldn't talk once I found out it was her. How sad, but I understood how she thought.

I called Janet to ask if the staff had phoned her, but she said they hadn't. We both wondered why not. Obviously, Mom had needed one of us to talk to, and although it wouldn't have been a pleasant call, at least Janet could have calmed her down. We figured that perhaps Mom had settled down on her own after her initial moment of anxiety. That sometimes happened.

All the same, I was thankful that we did make it out of our snowy driveway after all. It was clear Mom needed some attention.

The more I thought about it, the more I realized how wonderful it was that God saw His daughter in distress and then He made sure we got there to comfort her. And not only did I get to sit at the feet of my mother and reflect with her about Jesus, I got to appreciate the peace of God in the process.

Be Open to God's Direction

Life certainly has its ups and downs, and we must understand that and be prepared for both. I love a saying that I learned when our two boys were small, and David was working long hours to support us: "This too shall pass." No matter how difficult the situation, there will always be a cloud with a silver lining and proof that a new day comes every 24 hours.

Talking to God

Father, I often wish I could wave a magic wand to make everything better, but of course, I cannot. However, You are there with me every step of the way. May I always be aware of Your presence and lean heavily on You. Amen.

Wisdom

Let the words of my mouth and the meditation of my heart
Be acceptable in Your sight, O Lord,
my strength and my Redeemer.
Psalm 19:14

Mom has always had a few favourite sayings. The one she favoured the most to her daughters growing up was: "When you're looking for a peach, you don't go into a lemon grove." She meant this as advice for finding a good husband, and all three of her girls listened and each of us found a peach at our church. In fact, ten years after Daddy died, Mom, too, found her own peach at the same church. Even our son, Nathan, found Tanya and our other son, Matthew, found Sarah. The whole family have their own special peaches. Can't beat that!

For a few years, Mom had wanted to go home to Heaven. Life as she knew it was stripped away when Ken's mind became muddled and had to be put into a nursing home. Then, when she, too, had to move into long-term care it was hard. She cried when Ken didn't recognize her and rejoiced when he did. Of course, her mind was slipping too and that gave her great distress.

Many times, when Janet and I listened to her cry about how awful life was, we'd actually prayed and asked God to please release her from this life and take her home to be with Him. But those prayers were not answered immediately. And I believe I knew why.

God knew that it was in His plan for me to write a devotional for caregivers and those last few years spent in the capacity of being a caregiver, yielded pure gold. Plus, it was a learning experience for me. It's good to know we are not alone in our journey, and, because of our experiences, we can help each other going through similar trials. I used to take a paper and pencil with me whenever Mom and I were together and jot down the things that I wanted to share; things that might help others who care for loved ones. My notes turned out to be a real blessing as my manuscript started to take shape.

Mom likely never knew what her life was accomplishing as she fought her battles with dementia, but I am glad that God didn't answer our heart-felt prayer about releasing Mom from her earthly prison. She still had work to do on earth. After all, Father *does* know best!

Finding Gold in Trials

There is much wisdom to be found in the elderly. Most of these dear ones lived through the Depression and World War II and more. They knew what it was to do without or to make do with what was available. Take time to talk to someone and to really listen to their story. You'll both benefit from it.

Talking to God

Father, I thank You that You alone know my complete story from beginning to end. Guide me to someone who needs to share their story, and may it be a blessing to all. Amen.

Cry for Help

The Lord is good, A stronghold in the day of trouble;
And He knows those who trust in Him.
Nahum 1:7

"Oh Nancy. You just have to come. I am so messed up and I couldn't even eat any lunch. I need you so bad. PLEASE come! I need you!"

How do you turn down a heart-cry like that from your anxious mother?

I told Mom that David and I were eating our lunch, and that she should go lie down for a while. But she wasn't having any of that.

"I did have a nap this morning," she said. "But it didn't do any good. I really need you Nancy."

I told Mom that I would try to come, but I also advised her to lay down and have a nice nap.

"Okay, I'll do that but promise me you'll come. I need you!"

That did it. Mom's pleading got to me once again.

David didn't want me to go because he couldn't come. He had a badly bruised rib and wasn't up to driving. But I felt I had no choice. I finished my lunch, bundled up warm, and headed out.

First, I had to shovel the six feet of snow off our steps (maybe it was six inches, but it still was a *lot* of snow.) Then I cleaned off the car and rammed my way through the snow drifts in our driveway. The roads weren't too bad, but not great, but I pressed on. I stopped at the Elmira Deli for some fresh rolls and a cinnamon bun and arrived in Mom's room to find her sound asleep.

Normally I would have let her sleep, but, by gum, she's the one who got me out in all the snow, and besides, I had summer sausage, homemade beets, fresh rolls, and the cinnamon bun and all, so I woke her up. It took a bit of shaking, but she finally opened one eye.

"Nancy, what are you doing here!" (*what am I doing here?)* I told her about her weepy phone call and that I had some lunch for her because she didn't eat hers. I got her out of bed and helped her into her chair and put the tray with all the goodies laid out in front of her.

It seemed Mom was having a lucid moment. She didn't remember calling me and felt awful that she'd demanded that I come. I told her that most of the time we didn't come running because we'd learned that the dementia would subside soon and that she'd forget she even called us. But I was concerned that it sounded serious.

I told Mom that I'd given Janet a call before I left to see if she had planned on visiting her, but she had said that with the high winds, their driveways kept closing in and they hadn't had much choice other than sitting tight. Hank had hurt his back shoveling the other day and couldn't help either. I totally understood, and bravely went to help Mom, only to find out she was perfectly fine, thank-you very much!

Mom had a hard time with what she did, but she mentioned that she'd often get us a cup of cocoa late at night when we asked for it, and the relatives all thought she was spoiling us rotten, so perhaps this is balancing the scales.

The drive home was awful. It started to snow again, and the wind was fierce. I was thankful to finally see our house. Janet just laughed when I phoned her and said, "Nancy, you should know better."

"But it sounded serious!"

My smart older sister said, "It always sounds serious, but we know it passes."

I had to agree. Next time, I won't be so quick to jump, for as they say, experience is the best teacher! But it did sound serious.

Choose Wisely

It sure is tough to see someone hurting, especially a dementia patient—especially your mother. Even though we know it will pass and the person would not likely remember the incident at all, we still feel responsible. There is a fine line. We need wisdom to know when to help and when to wait until the dementia fog lifts. Some days it is hard to figure out the best thing to do.

Talking to God

Lord, I know I cannot always be there for the one I care for even if they live under my own roof. I still have to live my life and You totally understand that. Give me wisdom to know what to do in all situations, for I cannot do it on my own. Amen.

Cute Mother

The Lord your God in your midst, The Mighty One, will save;
He will rejoice over you with gladness,
He will quiet you with His love,
He will rejoice over you with singing.
Zephaniah 3:17

Mom was so cute this morning. Winter had been playing havoc, but we managed one good day out of the week. We'd planned on taking Mom out for breakfast if the weather cooperated, so Janet and I met at Mom's room. We helped her put on extra layers so she would stay warm. Then we helped her into Janet's car.

"I hope I don't talk too loud when we're there," Mom said.

We hadn't heard that comment before. Janet and I just looked at each other and smiled. The waitress seated us in a nice corner table.

Out of the blue Mom said, "I can't go to restaurants anymore you know."

Janet and I both chimed in, almost in unison.

"Mom, you're at a restaurant!"

Mom just looked at us blankly.

Well into the meal, I put some strawberry jam on Mom's toast as Janet and I continued talking.

"I need some more of that red stuff on my toast," Mom said a few minutes later.

I put some on her toast. She only had crusts left but still asked for more "red stuff" but I had to tell her that she ate it all.

"Was it me that ate it all?" She snapped back, a little indignant, "I don't think so!"

Uh, yea Mom, you did.

While we were finishing our coffee, Mom said, "I couldn't hear much of the conversation, but what I did hear was (long pause) I forget!"

All three of us laughed.

"My hearing and sight may be going, but my taster still works!"

Good medicine is all this laughter.

When we were in the car on the way back, Mom spotted Janet's purse.

"How did the green purse turn grey?"

For some reason, Mom had always made a fuss about *my* green leather purse. She was thinking Janet's purse was mine. We tried to explain that this one was not my purse.

"You mean you don't share a purse?"

"Mom likes my purse better than your purse, Janet," I said, in a sing-song kind of voice. Mom smiled.

Later, back in her room, Mom went on and on about how she liked Janet's boots, so I guess we were even. Janet didn't even go "na-na-na-na-na." She's a better person than me.

We visited Mom for a while.

"I feel so sorry for you girls to have to listen to my same old crap."

Janet and I laughed at what Mom had said. Mom would have never said, "crap" when we were growing up. She's turned into a regular potty-mouth!

Before we left, Mom gave her departing blessing.

"God's going to reward you for all you're putting me through!"

She realized what she said and added, "That didn't come out quite right."

We all laughed again.

Happy Days Are Here Again

What a joy it is when things are happy, peaceful, and wonderful. Because life isn't always this way, we must grab hold of the good times with abandon and rejoice in them. These times are what we can remember when things aren't going well; when there are heavy loads and problems that seem to be more than we can handle. Reach into your memory bank and let the sunshine of those times flood your heart and give you a lift.

Talking to God

Thank You for the good times, Father God. Sometimes I fear there is no light at the end of the tunnel, and then suddenly, something good happens that lifts my spirit and I know that they are from You. May I not forget all the goodness around me and the blessings that You pour over me. Thank You. Amen.

Not a Place for Old People

These things I have spoken to you, that in Me you may have peace. In the world you will have tribulation; but be of good cheer, I have overcome the world.
John 16:33

"They don't know how to take care of sick people here!"

Mom's greeting wasn't exactly a warm one. She was sitting in her lazy-boy chair wearing her nightgown and a light blanket. When she saw me, I could immediately tell that something wasn't right just by her body language. I laid my coat on the bed. David walked in but she didn't seem to notice.

"What's wrong Mom?"

She moaned.

"It happened at breakfast, and no one helped me."

"What happened?"

Mom paused and then said, "I don't know. But what I do know is that I don't belong here!"

"Well, Mom, where do you belong?"

She paused again

"I don't know, but they aren't equipped here."

I patiently explained that they have nurses and a doctor on staff and that they are very professional. But she wasn't buying it. She slumped in her chair. I knew I had to get her mind off her troubles.

"Mom do you remember going out for breakfast on Friday?" I tried to sound upbeat.

She did sit up a little straighter and admitted that she remembered. She told me she remembered it being a "yummy breakfast." I focused on some good things that she could see around her. I pointed out her gorgeous private room with a beautiful view of the front walk where she could watch people coming and going. I reminded her about the bush right outside her window where birds sit and sing often.

David asked to be excused so he could go into the common room where there was a Gaither Video playing, so it was just Mom and me. I shared a few of the comments from friends on social media about how much they loved her and how many are helped because of all our experiences.

Although she couldn't quite grasp it, I know it made Mom glad her life had some meaning. I also told her how easily I can write funny things because of our family.

"We had so much fun Mom, and we didn't mind sharing embarrassing stories as long as they made people laugh, didn't we?"

"Oh yes, the more embarrassing the better" Mom said. I looked at her smiling face and marveled, wondering how such an introverted lady could have such a wild sense of humour. Bottom line—laughter was a big part of family and, even though it's hard to explain, Mom would come out of her shell to tell a funny story. We never thought anything about the irony of it. Quite a heritage, eh?

Mom and I chatted back and forth for about an hour and a half. As I was getting ready to leave, Mom said, "David, you can come out of the bathroom now!" I guess she thought he was in there the whole time!

So, David, come out of the bathroom already and take me home!

Don't Worry, Be Happy

We all have days where nothing seems to go right, where we don't like where we are, but have no idea where we should go to make us happy. Life isn't all roses and sunshine for us. For those struggling with dementia or other illnesses, it is even worse. This is where patience comes in. Sometimes, just listening is all we have to do.

Talking to God

Father, You see me when I am happy, sad, angry, disappointed, jealous, rejoicing, or just plain out of sorts. Nothing I do or say can make You turn Your back on me or stop You from loving me. Help me to extend that same grace to others. Amen.

Memory Problem

A merry heart does good, like medicine, …
Proverbs 17:22a

Mom never fails to give me new material for my book. Each time I see her or talk to her on the phone, I wonder how she could possibly come up with all the funny stuff, but she does. You gotta applaud her for her originality!

When Mom first saw me this morning, she said, "Oh Nancy, my mind is so bad" (three times in a row.)

"I know Mom. It's been like that for a long time."

I've told her that before, but this time she added a little extra zing.

"Well if my mind has been so bad, why don't I know that?"

I had to laugh and soon she was laughing along too.

"You don't know your mind is bad, because your mind is bad!" I said.

We both laughed again.

Mom said, "It's time for me to—. She paused and used hand signals. "You know—."

I answered that I didn't know.

"What is it time for you to do?" I looked her straight in the eye.

"I forget!" Mom said amid gales of more laughter.

Janet arrived to help get Mom dressed and ready to head out for breakfast to our regular restaurant.

When we arrived at the door, the hostess recognized us and gave us a warm welcome. She led us to a table and served us our coffee—two regular, and one decaf. We all agreed that it tasted extra special because of the dreary day.

"My mother had it so hard," Mom said as we were eating.

Janet and I agreed that grandma did have a hard life. Then she wailed a little too loudly.

"My poor Mom didn't have any daughters."

We told her that grandma had four daughters and she was one of them. It came as quite a surprise. Janet and I suppressed a giggle, but Mom just carried on enjoying her eggs.

One of Mom's favourite lines is, "I'm so glad I had daughters and not sons."

We don't usually comment, but this time Janet said, "Mom, every time you say that, it's not nice for Nancy because she has two sons."

"And I love my two sons to death!" I added with a smile.

"Did they die?"

At first, Janet and I corrected her and assured her that they were very much alive, until we realized that she made a funny. Good one Mom!

Janet came back with, "I may have two daughters, but they are both far away, so it doesn't help me much!"

We explained that our sons were married to wonderful gals and that our daughters-in-law were precious and were good to us. Mom knew them all, so she had to agree.

After our discussion about family, she said she loved her breakfast but then made an announcement.

"This will be the last time you have to take me out," Mom said.

She often said this at the end of our outings. We simply went along with it, knowing that soon she'd give us hints like, "You used to take me to Joe's for breakfast, right? I really liked that." So, we planned yet another trip and scheduled it with Heritage House and each other. But we held off telling Mom right away.

Funny thing is, she always called the restaurant that we go to regularly, "John's" or "Joe's." It's called "Harvest Moon," which, as you will notice sounds nothing like John's or Joe's!

Another fun time with our sweet, adorable mother.

A Good Time was Had by All

I've heard that a belly laugh is like in internal jog, and those of us who greatly enjoy a good belly laugh, heartily agree. We feel cleansed somehow on the inside and can carry on with a lighter heart. Never pass up an opportunity to laugh, for it does indeed do good like a medicine, and it has no ill side effects!

Talking to God

When you created humans, God, you gave us the ability to laugh. No other creature can laugh like we can, and You did that on purpose because You knew how good it would be for us. Help me not to look at everything with gloom and dread, but rather search out the lighter side of life. It will do me and those around me, the world of good, and You will smile along with me. Amen.

Organized Mother

But the Lord is faithful, who will establish you
and guard you from the evil one.
2 Thessalonians 3:3

I'd been thinking a lot about all the good qualities our Mama had and it brought me joy and peace. Although Mom could no longer organize, I was thankful that she passed that trait on to me. I had Mom's gift of organization and *loved* to get my hands on anything that is out of order and to put it in its proper place (take David for example ... just kidding, Honey.) Years ago, when our son Nathan was a project manager of a renovation company, he asked me to organize his office and I did such a good job that a professional came in later and made a fuss about it. I'm bragging here, but it did feel good to hear his accolades.

One time my sisters and I were talking about how Mom labelled everything.

"When Mom dies, we'll have to put a label on the casket saying, *body*," Janet said.

We all roared, including Mom.

All Mom's dresser drawers and kitchen drawers were filled with small boxes cut down and labeled with masking tape. I imagine she went through rolls and rolls of the stuff, and many black magic markers to get all her jobs done. Even her medicine cabinet had labels on everything. It didn't matter how obvious it was to anyone else, she did it her way.

When she still lived at St. Jacobs Place retirement home, she loved her Red Rose tea, and would faithfully take her own tea bag down to the dining room and just ask for hot water. Anyone who's seen a Red Rose tea box, knows it is bright red with Red Rose in huge white block letters, but true to form, Mom put a piece of masking tape over the white Red Rose words, and she put Red Rose tea in her own handwriting.

Mom was the best person to pack boxes during a move. Each box was labeled carefully so we knew exactly what was in each one and to which room it should be moved. This made the transition much easier. We never laughed at her labelling then!

In her later years, Mom's need for organizing, meant that she often threw things out that she needed. Sometimes things disappeared mysteriously. She hated clutter, and towards the end, most of her drawers were empty.

We All Have Quirks

It is easy to laugh at other's quirky habits, but none of us is exempt. Although it is fine to make fun of someone with good humour, we must be careful that we don't go over the line and actually hurt the other person. We were fortunate that Mom had a great sense of humour and would laugh along with us.

Talking to God

Oh God, I know I am not perfect. I have plenty that I need to work on in my life; maybe even some things that I don't even know about. In some families something might be hilarious, in others it could be deemed painful. Please give me a sensitivity to know the difference. I certainly do not want to wound anyone with my words or actions. Amen.

To God Be the Glory

I will praise You, for I am fearfully and wonderfully made;
Marvelous are Your works,
And that my soul knows very well.
Psalm 139:14

One time when we were visiting Mom, we could see that she was tuckered out, but just before we left, David and I sang a hymn.

To God be the glory, great things he has done!
So loved he the world that he gave us his Son,
Who yielded his life an atonement for sin,
And opened the life-gate that we may go in.[10]

Mom sang right along, but her next question was a puzzle.

"Will they remember me?"

When I asked who she meant she replied, "The nurses." I assured her that they would remember her, and all of her family would too. Then I reminded her about the book I was writing about her.

"Be sure and give God all the glory!"

That was my Mama in a nutshell. She faithfully served God who she loved with all her heart. She wanted it known that He was the One who should get the praise.

Right after that solemn moment, with a little grin, she gave us the news that she tooted.

"You just toot away Mom!" David chimed in. "Can you toot a tune?"

I was laughing too. She thought David was a funny fellow. I rang Mom's call bell and two staff members arrived to take Mom to the bathroom. They asked her first.

---

[10] Fanny J. Crosby 1820-1915. Public Domain; hymnary.org

"Okay," she said.

"Your Mom is so adorable and compliant. She just goes along with whatever and is cute as a button," one of the girls said.

This made my heart happy, and I told Mom after they left that the nurses liked her. She just sweetly answered, "That's good."

What a precious soul my Mom is.

Songs Can Help

We have found that songs can reach a person in dementia more than almost anything else. If a person was raised in church, they'll most likely remember the words to hymns, even though they don't recall what they had for breakfast. If you can, find out what music your charge loves and sing along with them. It just might bring you both great joy.

Talking to God

Father, thank You for giving me the ability to sing and to enjoy listening to someone else sing, too. I know You delight in hearing my *joyful noise*. Guide me so that I can bring sunshine into the lives of others using the gift You have given me. Amen.

Peace, Beautiful Peace

Grace to you and peace from God our Father
and the Lord Jesus Christ.
2 Corinthians 1:2

Mom was cute today although she didn't realize it. When we walked into her room, she had her eyes closed. I opened her drapes and that caused her to look up. A lovely smile came over her face when she saw me. She is cared for and comfortable. God certainly blessed her for all her years of faithfulness to Him, and it was a comfort knowing she was well taken care of at Heritage House and had no pain.

Janet and I both agreed that Mom was more peaceful than she'd been in years. We believed that she had slipped a bit deeper in dementia and no longer worried about her mind and what she couldn't remember, and this made us truly thankful.

As I sat and watched her slip into sleep, I stroked her hair and recalled how bravely she carried on after daddy died when she was only 37, and daddy only 39. Daddy had had "moods" where he wouldn't speak for days at a time, yet Mom never complained. In fact, when daddy would come out of those moods, she'd act like nothing happened and carried on until the next "silence" came. She taught us to forgive quickly and stay happy and that is a lesson that I learned and still practice today.

On Mom's wall was a frame with many pictures of our family that our sister Jane put together. Jane was the creative one and, in the middle of the collage of pictures she made for Mom, was this verse: "Thank You God for all Your blessings to me and my family. For the strength You give me each day and for all the people around me who make my life more meaningful." (and Jane added) "especially Jane." We all hooted over that last line.

It was difficult to watch Mom waste away, but she was at peace and not in pain, so that made all the difference.

Peace is important

There are different stages in dementia or Alzheimer's. Times when the patient is overwhelmed with fear, anxiety, and even anger, so if peace does come, we should take comfort in that and dwell on the good times and try to forget the bad. It's not easy, but with God's help, we can concentrate on what is wholesome and good and it will lift our spirits and those we love as well.

Talking to God

Dear Jesus. How I thank You for peace. Your Word has many passages of Scripture that urge me to seek peace and that is what I surely want to do. There are so many outside reasons why peace isn't possible, but I am told not to dwell on these, but to look into Your eyes and accept Your peace. Thank You for this peace which passes all understanding. Amen.

Going Back in Time

I remember the days of old; I meditate on all Your works;
I muse on the work of Your hands.
Psalm 143:5

I reminded Mom about the time Janet and I were in a car accident. March 1965 was a day etched in my mind. I spent five days in St. Mary's Hospital. I had been sitting in the front seat when the car we were in hit a parked car. My head went through the windshield. I ended up with 42 stitches on my face. For years after, tiny shards of glass would come out of my face and it would hurt! However, as my doctor said, "Better out than in." He was so right. Mom was a widow for only four months when this happened, yet she faithfully came up to see me every day I was in the hospital. Oh how I eagerly looked forward to her visits.

Mom's mind was clearer than it had been in a long time. We had a good chat, but then I noticed she got very tired. I asked two Personal Support Workers to help her into bed so she could have a nap. As soon as she hit the pillow, she sighed and fell asleep. I covered her gently and sat on the bed for a bit. I marvelled at her lovely face and held her hands. I remembered those beautiful hands when they'd touch my forehead whenever I had a fever, or when she would hold my head when, as a child I was bent over a toilet vomiting. I remembered her soothing touch when I was that little scared girl in hospital.

I was blessed with so many beautiful memories of Mom's love and tender care, and it was special to visit those times once again, to talk to her and to thank her. Precious times indeed.

Dwell on Good Memories

No matter what our experiences of life have been, there are always good memories to focus on. We can't change the past, but we can enhance the present by remembering good things. They don't have to be huge, just something that gives you a warm-happy feeling. If possible, it would help if you shared it with the one in your care and give them a lovely memory too.

Talking to God

Thank You Father for happy memories. I realize that some of us have more happy memories than others, but if I can't think of anything good, I ask that you bring a memory back into my consciousness that will cause me to smile. Amen.

Sing a Song of Praise

But if anyone loves God, this one is known by Him.
1 Corinthians 8:3

One time when I went to visit, Mom was in the activity room. But she wanted to go to her room, so I wheeled her back. She kept repeating how wonderful it was to see me and how happy it made her feel. I had tears in my eyes as we traversed the hallway. Once we got to her room, I sat in the love seat and put Mom's wheelchair in front of me and we had a nice chat. I told her again that my many friends from all around the world are very interested in how she's doing and she admitted that it was hard for her to understand why they cared so much, but I could tell she was pleased about it.

Another time, Mom was in the dining room when I arrived after lunch, so I knelt down and touched her shoulder. She opened her eyes right away and gushed, "Oh Nancy. It's so wonderful to see you" over and over as I stroked her arm and replied that I was happy to see her too. We just soaked in the love.

I especially enjoyed the times when Hank and Janet and David and I were visiting Mom together in her room. Inevitably we'd begin singing beloved hymns or choruses and Mom would often quietly sing along with us. We sang in three or four-part harmony and often had people thank us for our mini concert. Some staff and visitors admitted they thought it was the radio or a C.D. and were surprised that it was live.

One time we were truly enjoying our time of singing and ready to keep going, but Mom said, "Well that was a good song to end on." (Hint, hint) We kissed her goodbye and left laughing all the way back to our cars.

We guessed Mom had had enough and wanted to sleep so we took it all in stride. Only our sweet Mama could get away with that.

Sometimes, Enough is Enough!

There are times when the ones we care for are simply tired and want to be left alone. This can hurt those who made the time and the effort to visit, but we also must recognize that the ones we care for may have other things going on in their minds that causes them to act this way. The best response is simply to give a loving hug goodbye and carry on with your day. The person will probably forget they even said anything, so no sense feeling bad, even for a second.

Talking to God

Jesus, You knew rejection. Many of the leaders tried to trick You and harass You, but that did not change You in any way. I must learn to let go of any hurts that inevitably happen, for often my loved one doesn't even realize the hurt that has happened. May I use Your example to simply keep on loving. This is the best way, for it is Your way. Amen.

Loving Heavenly Father

Let Your mercy, O Lord, be upon us,
Just as we hope in You.
Psalm 33:22

Mom wasn't in her room when David and I arrived late one afternoon. One of the staff saw us looking for her and pointed to the nurses' desk. There was Mom in her wheelchair, looking very dejected.

When the nurse saw me, she said, "Flo, your daughter is here to see you. Isn't that nice?" I knelt down before her and Mom started to cry and wailed the familiar, "Oh Nancy!"

We hadn't heard that in quite some time. When I gently asked what was wrong, she sobbed a little.

"Things are so bad that I can't even begin to tell you."

I wheeled Mom into the hall, and she cried louder.

"You're not leaving me, are you?"

My heart broke and I touched her shoulder, assuring her that I wasn't leaving. I told her we were going to the sunroom so we could talk. Once we were there, I again asked what was wrong and when she repeated her complaint of how bad things were, I realized that a dementia fog had settled in again.

Again, it hit me that God knew Mama was in distress. He understood she needed us at exactly that moment. It was the first time we'd ever visited her that late, yet His timing was perfect. I held her hands.

"You know Mama, God knew that you were struggling. He made sure we got here at just the right time."

Mom thought about that. I watched as she mulled it over.

"Why should God care about little old me?"

I assured her that God saw her as His beautiful daughter who had loved and faithfully served Him all her life. I reminded her how He made sure we got there when she needed us most. We both marveled at that truth and then began singing a song my sisters and I often sang.

"My Heavenly Father Watches Over Me."[11]

David joined in with his lovely tenor and we sang some more. Soon she was tired, so I wheeled her into the dining room and assisted her with her lunch. Right after, I took her back to her room and stayed until a PSW came in to get her ready for bed.

Our Heavenly Father truly *does* watch over us and that fills me with awe and thanksgiving.

Trust Your Instincts

There are many times that God is speaking to us telling us to either go somewhere, do something, say something, or call someone. If we make the choice to listen to His still small voice, He will guide us and it will be perfect. We don't have to have extra-ordinary powers to hear His voice, just a willing heart to be still and hear and obey.

Talking to God

Heavenly Father. It thrills me to know that You are everywhere at the same time, which means that You alone know when I am needed most by those around me. You see when my loved ones or those in my care are struggling, and Your timing is always right. Help me indeed to listen to your voice and respond, for You know best. Amen.

[11] Public Domain

Family

The eternal God is your refuge, And underneath are the everlasting arms; …
Deuteronomy 33:27a

Recently, my Uncle Ron and his wife Lois, met David and me at Heritage House. Mom was in the sunroom enjoying the live music of a sweet gal with a guitar, so the four of us waited in the activity room for her until it was over. It was hard for us to imagine that Mom seemed like she was at death's door three different times. Each time she rallied.

Ron and Lois had brought a candy bar that was only sold in the United States. It was one of Mom's favourites. So when they gave it to her and she tore open the wrapper, she amazed me by actually eating close to half of it. Mom's taste buds had been almost non-existent for a long time. I knew this was so, because she had turned down my delicious homemade fudge. She never did that, so we knew things weren't right.

It took some time for Mom to recognize who Ron and Lois were, but once she did, she was thrilled. After a brief visit, she grew tired though, so we wheeled her back into her room and put her into bed for a nap. Before Mom nodded off, she turned to Ron.

"What happens next?" she asked him. Ron admitted that he didn't know.

"Well what good are you?" Mom said.

He laughed and answered, "Not good for much obviously!" Lots of laughter ensued.

She was ready for a nap, so we kissed her and said our goodbyes. What a lovely family day it turned out to be with our Mama.

Family is Important

If your loved one or charge has family, it is important that you try to get them to visit and interact. Our lives can get busy, but there's nothing quite like family. Most of the time, it will be a visit down memory lane and that makes everyone young again. It's well worth the effort.

Talking to God

Oh Father, You created families. Of course, my family is not perfect, but there is something about being related that causes a bond that is special. May I overlook any hurts or slights or misconceptions that are prevalent, and reach out if possible, to bring as many together as we can. Heal any wounds so I can be whole and happy again. Amen.

Happy Mom

... that you may proclaim the praises of Him who called you out of darkness into His marvelous light; ...
1 Peter 2:9c

Mom was in top form when we arrived. We found her in one of the common rooms sitting at a table with the activity director. Mom had a large print *Chicken Soup for the Soul* book on her lap. She was happy to see us and told the staff member, over and over, "This is my daughter and my son-in-law." So cute.

"Your mom asked me to teach her how to read, but I soon found out that she already knew how to read," the activity director said, with a twinkle in her eye.

We all had a good chuckle about that. I wheeled Mom out into the hall and we just sauntered to the other end, heading to the sunroom. A family was seated there, but they invited us to come in and we had the nicest visit. Two brothers and a daughter-in-law were visiting their mother, Grace. Grace had lived in the same retirement home as Mom before moving to Heritage House. I asked how many children Grace had. To my surprise I found out that she had nine. I was impressed! We chatted and laughed a lot until it was time for lunch. I wheeled Mom into the dining room and got her settled.

Nothing out of the ordinary happened, but it turned out to be a beautiful and informative morning. After all, it's not every day you find out your mother can read!

Read out Loud

I wonder if we ever outgrow the love of someone reading to us. There is something special about hearing a story read with inflection and expression. Find something that interests the one you care for and, if they are interested, read out loud to them. You may both benefit from it.

Talking to God

Oh God, You have given me the ability to read and there are so many excellent books out there for me to explore. Your Holy Word is at the top of the list, and I thank You for the freedom to have as many copies of the world's best seller as I want. Not everyone is so fortunate. Show me what other books would be appropriate and may I bless others as well as myself. Amen.

Niagara Falls

But if we walk in the light as He is in the light, we have fellowship with one another, and the blood of Jesus Christ His Son cleanses us from all sin.
1 John 1:7

Our sister Jane made a beautiful collage of pictures for Mom years ago and it hung on the wall across from her bed. One was a photo of us three girls and Mom standing in front of a realistic mural of Niagara Falls. Looking at that particular photo, brought back some wonderful memories.

At the time, we had been heading to the outside elevator of the Skylon Tower, looking forward to a delicious meal in the revolving restaurant. It had been sprinkling a bit, so we had an umbrella. Instead of just posing properly in front of the mural, like everyone else, Jane opened the umbrella and there we were huddled together against the mist from the Falls. The photographer thought it was a hoot! We made it up to the Skylon Tower and were seated in the restaurant.

Because there weren't a lot of diners at the time, we could sit there for two full rotations during our meal. We saw the beauty of the Falls and the magnificence of the city. What a vantage point; a gorgeous sight to behold! Looking at that photograph transported us back to a happier time with our mama when she was able to walk, and her mind was clear.

As we looked at another photo of Mom and Ken on the wall, more memories surfaced. We reminisced about the 25 years Mom and Ken spent in the condo. I reminded Mom about how we would often walk across the street to the fabulous Rockway Gardens, or bike on the Iron Horse Trail. We laughed at our grit and determination back then. If we couldn't walk on the trails because the weather was bad, we'd go up to the 12th floor of Mom and Ken's condo, walk the halls twice, and continue this way on each floor until we got to the basement. After that we would end up in their apartment for a nice cup of tea. We'd talk up a storm as we walked, and I'll always remember those hours fondly. So many wonderful memories that I can take out and look at any time I want. How grateful I was to Jane for preserving them.

Pictures Are Important

If you are able to find photos of the years gone by, take some time to look at them together. It will not only be a pleasant time, but it could draw your loved one back to what used to be, even for a short while. Win-win.

Praise God

Thank you, Lord, for photographs. The ability to freeze a moment in time has not been around all that long and I feel truly blessed as I look at the past, sometimes through rose-coloured glasses, but that's okay. What does matter is that it transports me back in time and hopefully brings a host of good memories. Help me to set aside moments to reminisce. Amen.

Wonderful Easter

... Why do you seek the living among the dead?
He is not here, but is risen!
Luke 24:5b-6a

It was a beautiful Easter Sunday morning and Mom was in a light sleep when we first came into her room after a glorious church service. She rallied quickly and we were rewarded with a warm welcome and heard over and over how good it was to see us. We mentioned again about how my friends from around the world loved her even if they'd never met her because of my posts and she smiled a pretty smile and was quite pleased.

She also mentioned, "I've been through the mill today I'll tell ya!" But she wouldn't elaborate.

However, later, she told us how two nurses had tried to help her to walk. We'd met those two therapists before, and they truly would like to see Mom walk again. She would, too. No wonder she was tired. When I told her that it was Easter Sunday, she said that she already knew it was Easter, and that she was hoping someone would stop by. Just then Hank and Janet surprised us by walking in.

We had a good visit and then took Mom's old hymnbook out and began singing songs about the resurrection. It was glorious. Mom however, made no bones about shutting it down after a bit for she'd had enough, and enough it was. We put the head of her bed back down, kissed her goodbye and told her to have a good nap. She fell asleep almost immediately.

On our way out, some of the nurses let us know how much they enjoyed the concert, again, that came from Mom's room. That made us feel good. Blessing others always feels good.

Rejoice!

It doesn't have to be Easter to remember and celebrate the Resurrection of our Lord and Saviour Jesus Christ. There are so many wonderful hymns and choruses about our Lord's resurrection. Enjoy today with abandon and know that God is with us each step of the way.

Talking to God

Jesus. How thankful I am that You did not stay dead in the tomb but arose on the third day. Over 500 people saw you alive, and Your disciples, who were devastated the day before, suddenly realized that You were who you said You were—God's Son, and death could not hold You. I rejoice that You are indeed alive. I truly serve a risen Saviour! Amen.

Life Isn't Always Easy

A bruised reed He will not break,
And smoking flax He will not quench; …
Isaiah 42:3a

At the beginning of our visit, Mom was delighted to see us, but once again, her list of problems surfaced. She couldn't seem to give me one specific example.

"There are just too many to even begin," she said.

Loosely translated, Mom meant she couldn't pinpoint any one incident. Of course, both David and I knew dementia blew things out of proportion in Mom's mind. Our hearts ached for her during those episodes.

I had brought along some pretty silk pansies, but she didn't seem to care, so I put them in her room and guided her wheelchair out into the courtyard. It was a bit cool. The sun was shining, and we saw some pretty daffodils in the flower beds, but Mom was still in a snit, so we didn't have much of a visit. Soon she looked like she was starting to fall asleep, so I pushed her back to her room and two of the Personal Support Workers helped her into bed. To her credit, Mom did settle down and said, "I know you girls can't come all the time and it's okay."

Times of Discouragement

There will be times when visits just don't go well, but we shouldn't be discouraged. After all, a dementia patient does not have control when something in their mind switches. That signals that they need our love even more. We can always hope next time will be better.

Talking to God

Oh Father. Even you experienced disappointment and rejection when You were on earth. Not everyone was nice to you, or even accepted You, yet you carried on. Help me to carry on and continue to love those in my care I pray. Amen.

Compliments Count

Jesus said to her, "I am the resurrection and the life. He who believes in Me, though he may die, he shall live."
John 11:25

Sometimes when we visit, Mom is in a bad mood. "Where have you been?" is not an isolated question. Hurtful statements such as, "It's been such a long time since you visited," or "I feel abandoned," are not uncommon greetings.

On those days, it is difficult, but because we know it is the dementia talking and not Mom, we try to change the mood.

Once David and I found Mom's hymnbook on her table and chose a few songs to sing. I sang the soprano while David offered his beautiful harmony, and Mom joined in. My precious Mama had her eyes closed during each song and somehow she looked like a saint to me. My heart tightened as I realized that she was more than ready to meet her wonderful Jesus of whom we sang. One day soon, she would see Him face-to-face. After singing for a while, Mom said something to me she'd never said before.

"Oh Nancy, you still have a beautiful voice."

Mom probably never mentioned it before because Janet, Jane, and I had been told over the years that we had beautiful voices. The Dubrick Sisters sang together on stage for many years. Janet and I still sing on stage with our husbands, so I guess it's no big deal in our family. Mom probably never thought of telling me how much she liked my voice.

Corny, maybe. But hearing those words from my mother, was like music to my ears.

David pushed Mom's wheelchair in the hall, while I held her hand.

"We enjoyed your singing and the doctor made quite a fuss over it," one of the nurses said. I'd noticed the doctor doing paperwork at the front desk near Mom's room but didn't realize they could hear us singing. The nurse's comments made us feel good. It is encouraging knowing that the ministry of song can occur even outside the walls of a church.

Mom would never know what a gift she gave me that day with that compliment,

"You still have a beautiful voice." It continues to ring in my ears. Thank you, Mama. And thank You, God for the wonderful gift of singing You gave us.

Share Your Encouragement

I have often thought something good of someone but failed to share it with them, and always regretted it. Every person needs to receive accolades. Even a small word of kindness can make their day, week, or even their year! Be free with your compliments and it will make you feel better about yourself too!

Talking to God

I thank you, Lord, that You love me, even when I don't deserve it. There are times, though, when I am able to make someone else's day by complimenting them. May I do this as often as I can. Amen.

Tough Times

Now may the God of hope fill you with all joy and
peace in believing, that you may abound in hope
by the power of the Holy Spirit.
Romans 15:13

Janet and I take turns so that Mom has a visitor almost every day, but we never know what "Mom" we're going to meet. One time when Janet arrived, Mom was in the activity room.

"You girls just leave me here and you have no idea what I've had to put up with. I should horsewhip you!" Mom yelled.

Janet took a deep breath and asked Mom if she'd like to go into her room. Mom gruffly answered in the affirmative. When they got there, Mom went on another rant about how she hated her room, and nothing was right. And, of course it was all our fault. Janet told me she sat on the couch and pulled Mom's wheelchair in front of her.

"What's wrong Mom?" she asked.

"There's so much I can't even begin," Mom said. It was her standard answer when she felt overwhelmed.

"Well, just give me one example."

Mom couldn't come up with anything, so Janet changed tactics. She turned the chair around and told Mom that it would be okay. Together they walked to the sunroom. They chatted and looked out the window, admiring the flowers and the birds. Soon Mom was tired and ready to go back to her room. When they were safely inside, Mom inhaled deeply.

"I guess this is a nice room and they really do treat me well here," she said, much to Janet's relief.

Because it was close to lunch, Janet stayed until a worker came in to help Mom into the bathroom. Mom insisted that Janet could go home. She was thankful that the meltdown was over, and Mom was herself once again.

When Angry Tirades Come

Life hurts when we are unfairly accused doesn't it? We try to remember that it isn't the person talking and dementia has taken over, but the sting is still there. Sometimes we can reason with our charge or change the subject, but sometimes we must just walk away. It may seem hopeless, but this is a time when we can calmly pray and ask God to intervene and calm the person down and then leave it with Him.

Talking to God

God, it hurts when I am doing my best, but nothing helps. You see the one that is in the grips of dementia and how I try my best to take care of her. There are times when there is little I can do except to leave her in Your care. Help me to trust that You know all things and have it under control. Thank you that You are with me 24/7 and I can trust You. Amen.

Meal Gone Bad

Wisdom and knowledge will be the stability
of your times, And the strength of salvation;
The fear of the Lord is His treasure.
Isaiah 33:6

I had it all worked out. David and I would pick up hamburgers, french fries, and ice cream treats after church for five. Mom, Hank, Janet, David, and I would enjoy our feast in the sunroom. With food bags in hand, we arrived. Hank and Janet were already there. To my dismay, Mom was in her wheelchair crying (not a great start). However, we were sure that she would perk up when she saw the hamburger and fries in front of her. She would normally dig right in. Didn't happen.

Even the ice cream treat didn't excite her. Then, I brought out the highlight of the meal—my very own delicious homemade rice-marshmallow squares. But to our dismay, she wouldn't touch them. Some days it just doesn't pay to get out of bed. Do you know what I mean?

Right from the start, Mom refused to eat unless Janet fed her and even then, she showed no enthusiasm whatsoever over anything. We noticed that her eyes looked dead. We urged Mom to eat and she asked where her food was. We pointed right at it, "I don't see it," Mom said.

We sadly realized, that for some reason, she truly didn't see it.

When we told one of our favourite Personal Support Workers, Jo, about Mom's eyes and how dead they looked, she said that she noticed the same thing. Jo also added something we didn't know. Apparently, dementia patients sometimes have what is called "scuba vision." Anyone who has gone scuba diving or even snorkeling and wears that mask, understands the limited vision and this is what seemed to be happening to Mom's eyesight. It made perfect sense and we thanked Jo for sharing that with us.

Mom began to fall asleep in her chair, so we cleaned up the "picnic" lunch and wheeled her to her room. Soon, two workers came in and put her to bed. She fell asleep almost immediately.

We started to feel sorry for ourselves but then thought of Mom. What must it have been like for her? Our hearts were heavy as we walked out to our cars.

Trying to Understand

We simply cannot fathom what is going on in the mind of a dementia patient. It must be horrible. It is important that we lovingly care for our loved one and forget about our own pain. It isn't easy, but the storm is real, and we must carefully and prayerfully ride it out.

Talking to God

Oh God. My heart can be so heavy at times for those I care for. Help me to understand. I pray that You will reach through the dementia fog and minister to their hearts. Nothing is too hard for You. Amen.

Changes Life Brings

Now godliness with contentment is great gain.
1 Timothy 6:6

It's a good thing we don't know the future. I am sure that none of the residents at the nursing home ever pictured themselves in such a place when they were young, healthy, and active with their families and careers.

One particular day I visited Mom at lunchtime, but she wasn't interested in eating; neither was she very happy. To lighten the conversation, I pointed to the lady on Mom's left who always carries her "baby" with her.

"That will be me someday." I gestured toward the lady cradling the baby doll.

Mom smiled and agreed that it did give many women comfort. As I was coaxing Mom to eat, I enjoyed talking to a worker who was feeding a few other residents. I'd never seen this gal before, so it was a delight to get to know her. We discussed how every one of us has a story. We talked about how none of us knows if we would end up in a nursing home. It was, indeed, a sobering thought.

Lunch was over. I wheeled Mom to her room and visited with her for a short time. Just before I left, I positioned her by the window so she could see outside. As I was driving out, I made sure I came as close to the outside window as I could to wave good-bye. She saw me and I loved it when she blew kisses back at me. I am so glad she had a nice view of the walkway so she could see all the visitors coming and going, which often kept her smiling and occupied.

Live for Today

We may not know what the future holds, but we know Who holds the future. All of us have so much to be thankful for. Take time today to count your blessings. Lay aside all your concerns and be thankful for what God has done for us. I do believe that you will feel better.

Talking to God

Only You know my future, Father. I must live one second, minute, hour at a time for that is how You created me. Obviously, You knew that I could not handle seeing into the future, so you gave me the gift of the present moment. Help me make the most of it I pray. Amen.

Thank God for Good Days

He loves righteousness and justice;
The earth is full of the goodness of the Lord.
Psalm 33:5

I was rewarded with a lovely, soft smile when Mom spotted me at noon today. David and I visited her right after church. We found her sitting at her table in the dining room, so I helped her with her food. The tomato soup went down well, but the main course, not so much. She tasted it and would not open her mouth for any more. I had her try her chocolate milk. Bingo. That was accepted. Then came the dessert cart. She liked the ginger cookie (dipped in her tea) along with a dish of chocolate ice cream. She let me know in no uncertain terms, though, when enough was enough.

I was happy to wheel Mama outside for a short time. It was a little chilly, but I had her wrapped in a blanket. She snuggled without a complaint while we enjoyed all that God made. We saw tulips, daffodils, bluebells, and a flowering tulip tree. The sky was blue, the clouds were fluffy white, the sun was shining, and the birds were singing. Mom even made a fuss about a lone dandelion poking its little head between the paving stones. It brought back memories of how she always made us aware of God's Creation. We were taught to literally *stop and smell the roses*, and we have carried on that beautiful tradition with our families to this day. Mom finally grew tired. We rang her bell and some Personal Support Workers came to help her to settle in her bed for a nap.

All in all, it turned out to be a better visit than I could have imagined, and I was content to leave Mom in the capable hands of the loving staff at Heritage House.

Treasure the Good Days

Ahhh…the good days. The times when things go according to plan and our loved one or our charge is in a delightful mood with no drama. These are the times we need to hide in our hearts and then remember to bring them out when the not-so-good times come. It is refreshing indeed.

Talking to God

How I thank You for all the pleasant times. You give me these times to help me make it and I am so appreciative. Remind me often of the good times so I don't get discouraged. Amen.

Personal Support Workers

Therefore comfort each other and edify
one another, just as you also are doing.
1 Thessalonians 5:11

"Oh, I'm so happy now!"

These were the beautiful words my "sleeping-beauty" Mama uttered when I sat on her bed and gently touched her shoulder. Mom gave me a beautiful smile. We talked until she said she needed to use the bathroom. I rang for a Personal Support Worker (PSW) to come and help. To my delight, one of our favourite PSWs was working so we began to talk as she went about her duties with Mom.

When I asked if she was getting together with her family at Easter, I discovered that this lovely gal doesn't come from a close-knit family, and many of them aren't speaking. She became especially dear to us, though. At one point she openly shared her difficult story with me, and I was very sad that she had to go through so many trials.

However, as she put it, "I am a different person since I found God in a real way and He is taking good care of me and my kids and I love my church and the family of God."

My respect for her quadrupled at that point, and I had to give her a hug. Just before she left, she reached out and hugged me again, and I had tears in my eyes.

Be Attentive to Others

Everyone has a story, and many do not mind sharing theirs if they feel comfortable with the person that shows interest. Even a little bit of history will draw you closer and give insight into why the person is the way they are. It may surprise you how people open up if they know you care about them. A little concern and compassion will go a long way.

Talking to God

God of the universe, You are the only One who knew me from conception, and thus You understand me better than I understand myself. May I show love and compassion to those who work so hard even though they are carrying heavy loads themselves. May I show the kindness and respect they deserve. Amen.

Loving Family

Blessed be the God and Father of our Lord Jesus Christ, who has blessed us with every spiritual blessing in the heavenly places in Christ,
Ephesians 1:3

David had a chance to play in a hockey tournament in Traverse City, Michigan. We had friends there, so we could stay with them. The catch was, however, that it was the Mother's Day weekend. It touched my heart that our oldest son, Nathan, urged us to go, assuring us that he would visit Mom in our stead. He promised to give us a detailed report. We packed up and headed south.

Apparently, Mom was awake when Nathan arrived, so he wheeled her down to see Ken. Nathan told me how Mom held Ken's hand and spoke lovingly to him. Nathan wrote down all the details so he could give me the whole story when we came home.

"I know you're having a hard time," Mom had said to Ken, "but I am filling in for you, Kid. You are my sweetheart and I love you."

Nathan had lots to write.

"I love you very much and you will always be my love, Ken. You may not be hearing me anymore, but I want you to know that I love you and am praying for you every day."

Does that not melt your heart? I think Nathan was touched, too.

Nathan told me that Grandma sometimes called him Matthew (his brother), or David, or even Grandpa. He didn't try to correct her. It made him smile. He wheeled Mom for some ice-cream and then back to her room. As Mom was eating her ice-cream and looking out the window, she asked Nathan if he could see the "grey car" from her room.

"Yes," Nathan said.

What he didn't know is that I had shown Mom our new silver car the last time we visited, and she had apparently remembered. Nathan got a chuckle when Mom said, "I think that's my grandpa's car."

Nathan told Mom that we were staying with friends in Michigan, and that we loved her very much. During their conversation he made sure to tell her that I always told them what a wonderful mother she was. That made her happy.

Nathan had a wonderful time with his grandmother and will remember it with great fondness. It truly worked out well for both grandson and grandmother.,

Do we have a great family or what?

Take Some Time for Yourself

No one needs to feel guilty for taking a vacation. Caregivers need a break. It is important to have "me" or "us" time to refresh and be energized as a caregiver once again. Another important thing is to forget your responsibilities for a time and trust that those who are filling in for you will do a great job. Perhaps they will appreciate your efforts even more.

Talking to God

Thank you for times of rest. You know that I can only carry burdens for a short time before I break, so You encourage me to stop and regroup from time to time. Help me not to feel guilty when I do take needed "me" time but to enjoy it to the full. Amen.

Hard to Watch Sometimes

Now to Him who is able to do exceedingly abundantly above all that we ask or think, according to the power that works in us, to Him be glory in the church by Christ Jesus to all generations, forever and ever. Amen.
Ephesians 3:20-21

When I arrived for one of my visits, two therapists were trying to get Mom to walk. But her legs just kept crumbling. The therapists finally gave up. I didn't let Mom know I was there and just watched as her legs buckled. I talked to the therapists after, and they shared that Mom walked a bit yesterday, but not today.

I knelt in front of Mama's chair and noticed her eyes seemed vacant. I'd only seen her look like that a few times before, and it was most unsettling.

"Hello Mom." I said with a happier voice than I felt.

Although she gave me a smile, Mom didn't say a word. I could see that something wasn't quite right but thought perhaps some fresh air would help. I got a blanket and her light coat, helped her on with it and off we went into the courtyard. It was a gorgeous, warm sunny day. I parked her chair in front of the beautiful tulip tree, but her eyes wouldn't focus. Nothing I said could get her interested. It broke my heart.

Times like that were tough. It was heartbreaking watching my precious Mama slowly slip away knowing there was nothing that I could do to stop it.

I cried on the way home.

Reality Hurts Sometimes

We've all been there as caregivers. Some days are good and happy when those we care about seem to be doing better, and then the bottom drops out and all seems hopeless. These are the times when we must "tie a knot and hang on" to the end of our rope. It is a comfort to know we are not alone, and do not have to carry the burden ourselves.

Talking to God

Sometimes life hurts, Father. You see me in my pain as I watch helplessly when the one I care about is suffering. I may not be able to do much about it, but You can. Not only can I run to You, but I can lay my burdens at your feet and know that you will help me carry them. It is a comfort to know you love me more than I could possibly understand and for that I am thankful. Amen.

In Someone Else's Shoes

The Lord is near to those who have a broken heart,
And saves such as have a contrite spirit.
Psalm 34:18

Our family was very thankful for the staff who worked tirelessly, often being required to do some not so pleasant jobs. Yet they did them with grace while maintaining the dignity of the residents. To show my gratitude, I decided to make some marshmallow rice squares for the staff, and a few for Mom. Many of the staff thanked me for them on my way out. I, in turn, thanked them for the wonderful job that they were doing. Most of them were kind, loving, and patient, and we owed them a huge debt of gratitude.

There was a staff member who was quiet and for some reason we didn't click right away. I wondered a little about her, so I prayed for her. The Lord seemed to say, "Nancy, you have no idea what her upbringing was like, nor what her situation is right now, but I do."

A wave of compassion for this woman overwhelmed me. God was right, for I did not know her story, therefore I could not judge. I determined to be extra kind to her and hopefully it made a difference.

On the day we dropped of the marshmallow treats, Mom was not herself, we discovered. She seemed angry with me for some reason. Even my marshmallow treats didn't cheer her. I tried my best to lighten things up, but she seemed to want to be grumpy and that was that. The Personal Support Workers were kind and came into the room to tell me it was time to take Mom to the bathroom and then she would be heading to the dining room for lunch. I felt a heaviness leaving Mom, but I needed to go. I kissed her goodbye and left.

But I couldn't get "my grumpy Mom" or that staff member off my mind. I was, however, glad that God placed prayer, instead of annoyance, on my heart that morning. I hoped it was just an off day for both of them and I also hoped that my marshmallow squares put a smile on both their faces later on.

Kindness Counts

Although it is difficult to be nice to someone who doesn't respond and act the way we would like, often those are the people who need our kindness the most. Only God knows why we behave like we do, and it is important to show God's love to all.

Talking to God

God, please bless all nurses and Personal Support Workers and staff and give them Your strength to carry on each day. Help me to love those who are struggling and to see how You can transform a person even through our inadequate efforts, for You can do anything. Amen.

Forgive Quickly

And forgive us our debts, As we forgive our debtors.
Matthew 6:12

I was so focused on getting to Mom's room that I didn't see her sitting in the hallway by the activity room. But she saw me. David called me back and said that Mom was in the hall and wondered why I hadn't seen her. Oh dear. How could I miss my own mother? I felt terrible and quickly went to her and apologized and all was forgiven. One of Mom's greatest qualities is that she can forgive quickly. She never was one to hold grudges, but she would forgive and move on. She showed us by example just how important this was. I tried to remember over the years, to forgive quickly, too.

Because it was close to lunchtime, I wheeled Mom into the dining room and tried to help feed her. She had no appetite, so it was a challenge to convince her to eat.

As I pushed Mom out of the dining room, I was once again thankful for all the good things my mama taught me. To love God, and to forgive easily. That has helped me greatly all through life. Forgiveness made sure that bitterness could not take hold and hurt me.

Soon I settled Mom into bed, and she looked so peaceful. *Sleep well my sweetheart.*

Easy to Say, "Forgive." Harder to Do

We have all been hurt in the past. No one gets off free from this trial. However, Jesus was very clear when He said that we must forgive. Forgiveness does not mean we are letting the other person off the hook, but it is saying, "You can't hurt me any longer with this." Forgiveness is for us. It sets us free from bitterness that can eat like acid. Do yourself a favour and forgive. If you can't forgive, ask God to help you and He will, because He knows how important it is to forgive.

Talking to God

Jesus, You were able to forgive those who tortured you mercilessly, stripped You, beat you, and hung You on a cross where You had to endure unbelievable pain and verbal abuse from those who wanted You dead. It was amazing that you could say, "Father, forgive them for they know not what they do," when I so easily hold a grudge because someone hurt my feelings. I have been hurt deeply in the past, but You always helped me to overcome the pain and now I try to make a concentrated effort to forgive. I need Your help Father, and You promised you would be there for me. Thank you. Amen.

Be Kind

And be kind to one another, tenderhearted, forgiving one another, even as God in Christ forgave you.
Ephesians 4:32

Mom was resting when I walked into her room, but she awakened when I opened her curtains. It was good to see her loving smile when she spotted me and then David, who followed behind. I sat on the side of her bed stroking her hair, telling her how much I loved her. As wc were talking, two workers came in and offered to put Mom in the wheelchair. My poor little Mama knew we were asking her to decide. Should she stay in bed? Or should she go in the wheelchair? It was adorable how she pondered it over and over as if it was monumental. Her mind wouldn't quite grasp what she should do. I finally helped her decide. I suggested she get into the wheelchair and then we would all go for a little stroll and perhaps we would go outside.

David and I walked her to the sunroom for a bit, then I returned to her room and grabbed her coat and a blanket. Then we took her outside in the sunshine. We sang some choruses, but then a chilly breeze came up.

"Time to go in!" Mom said, so we rolled her back inside and into the main common room.

A lady was playing hymns on the organ.

"Let's sing along, Mom," I said.

David and I joined in. We had arrived at the tail-end though and felt badly when she announced that she was finished and thanked everyone for coming. Total silence after that and David quietly said, "And the fans are going wild!" I couldn't help but laugh softly, but of course, Mom didn't get it.

I watched Mom's hands for a while. I pointed out to David how restless they were. She still had her blanket on her lap but kept pulling at the top and "worried it" like we used to say. Then she began to moan, repeatedly.

"Help me to be kind and loving," she kept saying. Then in a crystal-clear voice she suddenly said, "Did you check my suitcase?"

I wondered if she was telling us that she was ready to move on, but no amount of coaxing could get more out of her. We wheeled her back to her room and the two workers thought perhaps she needed to go to the bathroom and kindly took over. While they were taking her to the bathroom, I told them about Mom's prayer to be more kind and loving and they sweetly said, "Your Mom is always kind and loving."

That touched my heart. To be kind and loving is rather a good prayer, don't you think? I decided to make that my prayer too.

"Lord, please help me to be kind and loving too. Amen."

I was still learning things from my Mama.

Kind and Loving

What would it look like to be kind and loving? I believe one way would be to try to walk in the other person's shoes rather than to judge them for their bad or difficult behavior. Being kind and loving would be to give a smile, or a hug if it's appropriate. It could also mean to help someone with a heavy load or inquire as to how things are going. It doesn't take much to make someone else's day and I want to be that someone. How about you?

Talking to God

Lord, there is a song that says, "Let there be peace on earth and let it begin with me." I may be only one person, but if I do my share, I can be part of a mighty army of people who look for ways to help others. Amen.

When is Tomorrow?

Home Is Where the Heart Is

The name of the Lord is a strong tower;
The righteous run to it and are safe.
Proverbs 18:10

Mama acted so differently today. Sometimes she would make a statement that didn't make sense, and then she would nod off. We used to have such wonderful discussions, but those days were gone and sadly I had to accept that.

We had decided to take Mom outside, so I picked up a light blanket from her room just in case it still would be too cool for her and off we went. David pushed the wheelchair while I walked beside it, holding Mom's hand. I was surprised at her strength as she squeezed my hand over and over.

"There's no place like home. There's no place like home. There's no place like home."

Her repetition puzzled me at first, because Mom always stated that she only felt at home with her family. Perhaps our presence gave her peace and it felt like "home." She seemed content. Of course, I agreed with her. When we got outside, I put the blanket around her shoulders and arms and thought about the many times she must have done this loving action for me.

Mom told us often about the time daddy had bought her a beautiful baby pram. One of Mom's delights was to take her babies for long walks in the pram. She always loved to walk. Although I couldn't recall being in that buggy, I still got a sense of complete happiness thinking about it. How thankful I was for the loving memories I had of all our times together. We walked long distances, bicycled for miles, enjoyed gallons of tea together, and sat at Mom's table countless times to feast on her good cooking. And we always stopped and smelled the flowers along the way.

It's still hard to watch Mom on her downward spiral into dementia, but at least Mom knew we loved her and was "back home" every time we were with her.

Remember

If you know the one you are caring for well, try to remember the good days. The ones that give you a smile or a warm heart. It is easy to just see the confused person in front of you, but inside, they are whole and young. Treat them with the respect they deserve and you'll both benefit exceedingly because of it.

Talking to God

Oh Father. I do not know the future. I may be strong and healthy now, but that could change in a heartbeat. Help me to appreciate my life and see the good around me. There is suffering and pain yes, but You've given me the great outdoors, stars at night, and many days that are full of sunshine. May I dwell on these blessings. Amen.

But Mom!

The sun shall no longer be your light by day, Nor for brightness shall the moon give light to you; But the Lord will be to you an everlasting light, And your God your glory.
Isaiah 60:19

"I am so ready to be out of here!"

These were the words that Mama spoke when I entered the dining room and crouched beside her wheelchair while she was eating lunch. I think she either wanted lunch to be over with (she didn't eat much) or she was longing for life itself to be over.

I couldn't blame her for either sentiment. But still, my heart ached. We'd come directly from church that day. David and I planned to take Mom out to the courtyard and into the glorious warm sunshine right after she'd finished lunch. So, we did. After about 10 minutes we brought her back to her room.

"David, your butt is bigger than mine!"

We were taken aback for a few seconds but then peals of laughter rang out. Neither David nor I knew quite what to say after she uttered those words. Once we regained our composure, we wondered if it had something to do with Mom's couch.

Last week, Heritage House asked if we'd take the love seat out of Mom's room, because they needed to use a lift to take her to the bathroom. The love seat was in the way. So last Thursday, Hank, Janet, David, and I went there. David and Hank lifted the heavy couch and put it into our van. Mom was mostly sleeping as we rearranged her room. Occasionally she'd awaken, though, so we tried to explain why we were taking the couch out, but she didn't seem to care one way or another. The staff was pleased that they now had more room to carry out their duties. We told them that making their job easier was more important than our backsides!

Mom could have been thinking about the missing couch and the "butts" that used to sit on it, but we did have a good laugh over that one. Oh Mama, you are so adorable.

Feels Good to Laugh

Our body needs food, water, clothes, shelter, love, and most importantly—laughter. Truth is, we probably don't laugh enough. I heard about someone who was dying of cancer, and he asked for all the funniest old movies to be brought in. He laughed his way back to health with "Buster Keaton," "Laurel and Hardy," and "Abbot and Costello!" Take some time to look back at some old funny classics and you'll find yourself laughing again. It will do you the world of good.

Talking to God

How good it feels to laugh. Help me Lord to see the funny side of life and not just be serious all the time. May I search out good comedy that will tickle my funny bone and give me a new lease on life. Amen.

Birthday Musings

Now godliness with contentment is great gain.
1 Timothy 6:6

There's something about birthdays that causes one to ponder. My "pondering" took me back to the stories told of my birth. Mom had a normal pregnancy and was admitted to K.W. Hospital when her labour began. Nothing out of the ordinary, except when Mom began to hemorrhage. As soon as the doctors realized what was happening, they rushed her into surgery to do an emergency C-section. The placenta was coming out first. Placenta previa. Back then, it was touch and go as to whether mother or baby would survive with such a diagnosis, but we both made it. Had Mom not been at the hospital at that time, we both would have surely died.

As I was thinking about this, I realized how different life would have turned out for several people. Daddy could have become a young widower; Janet would have been motherless, and Jane would not have been born. There would have been no Dubrick Family singers or Dubrick Sisters trio. David would have married someone else (but she would have been mighty fortunate) and there would have been no Nathan, no Matthew, nor any of our grandchildren or future generations from our union. Not only that, but there would be no Nancy, and you would not be reading this devotional. No one would have ever heard my loud laugh. Now there's a scary thought!

Phew. I thanked God for making sure Mom and I both survived and for the life that God has given us.

When I was with Mom one day, I reminded her about our daddy and how he died young. I wanted to know if she remembered him well. I told her she was a very good mother. I asked if she remembered us girls and how we were well known as "The Dubrick Sisters." I was eager to find out if she remembered making our singing dresses. I reminded her how she faithfully came with us to all our singing engagements and how she would even choose songs she thought would go well with our voices. I thanked her for her support all through the years with our ministry and we both had tears in our eyes. It was quiet for a minute. Then I thought of a song she might like and sang it—over and over:

"Friendship with Jesus
Fellowship divine
Oh, what blessed sweet communion
Jesus is a friend of mine[12]."

I held Mom's hand until I was sure she was asleep, then gently kissed her and quietly left.

Memories

The past has been written, good and not-so-good. We can see things as they were, or perhaps we have re-written them to pretend things were better than they actually were. Regardless of our past, we cannot change it, but we can change our future because we control our attitudes and our actions.

Talking to God

Oh God. My times are in Your hands. I sometimes wish I could go back in time and right the wrongs or do things differently, but truth is, I cannot. Show me how to live the life You ordained for me. Guide my steps and clear my path. Help me to listen to Your voice so that I make right choices. Amen.

---

12 Public Domain

Perfect Peace

Behold, God is my salvation, I will trust and not be afraid; …
Isaiah 12:2a

I was pleasantly surprised to see Mom's eyes open when I walked into her room. Both Janet and I had been having trouble understanding Mom, even though we listened carefully. Today was no exception. She mumbled something, but I only caught the words "second husband." I knew she meant Ken, so I slowly told her that Ken's room was down the hall. She didn't show any understanding, so I picked up a nice picture of her and Ken that was on her dresser. She peered at it for a long time, but again, no recognition. Her face contorted. I wasn't sure if she was about to cry or scream. Turned out it was just a yawn. It was a relief to know she was just tired, not agitated. (Boring you, was I Mom?)

After a number of yawns, she mumbled.

"Do I have to …?" Even though I couldn't understand all of her question, I answered her, to the best of my imagination.

"No Mom, you don't have to do that. In fact, you don't have to do anything. Everything is all taken care of."

I could see her visibly relax and then she drifted off to sleep. I tearfully prayed and thanked God for my Mother who had loved and served Him all her life. I asked Him to keep all anxiety and fears away from her and to cover her with His peace. She had had an even temperament all through her life, and even the trauma of widowhood at 37 years of age didn't cause her to go over the edge. Simply put, she trusted that God would take care of her and her three girls, and He did.

When I realized Mom wouldn't be waking up for a long time, I kissed her and silently left the room with a prayer on my lips for God's protection over her.

Comfort

There are times when those we care for are anxious, and we cannot figure out what they are anxious about. This is when we can try to assure them that all is well, and that they have nothing to worry about.

Talking to God

Thank You for your peace. You are the "Peace Speaker" and I can trust you totally. Love and protect those in my care and show me how I can take care of myself as well, as that is important also. Amen.

Nice Birthday

My little children, let us not love in word
or in tongue, but in deed and in truth.
1 John 3:18

It was my birthday. Hank and Janet took David and me out for breakfast and we had a delightful time. After that, the four of us visited Mom. It was difficult for she was sitting in her wheelchair but seemed to be in a dementia fog and didn't recognize us. Janet tried to tell her that it was my birthday, but it didn't sink in. In fact, she didn't even look over at me, even though I was right in front of her. We wheeled her to her room and then Mom started to moan.

"What's wrong Mom?" I asked.

"I want it to be my birthday!"

Janet asked her why.

"I don't know!"

None of us knew whether to laugh or cry.

We then did what we love to do, and that was to sing one familiar song after another in three-part harmony. It felt like we experienced a little bit of Heaven right there in Mom's room. Although Mom didn't show much emotion, we were sure it touched her soul. I truly am a very thankful now 69-year-old woman, (who certainly doesn't feel her age) to have such a great family. It was a lovely way to spend my birthday. This would be the last one with my mama.

On the way out, the staff thanked us for the impromptu concert, and we could honestly say that it was our pleasure, for we loved nothing better than to sing.

What Are Your Talents?

Each one of us has gifts and talents. We know they are gifts and talents when we can do them with ease and with passion. This doesn't mean we don't keep improving our crafts, but a gift is a joy. It could be singing, or painting, or carving, or running, or speaking, or teaching, or even writing. The list is endless, but it is important to take time to engage in these things as it will refresh us to carry on and bless others in the process.

Talking to God

I am truly thankful that You have given me special talents. I pray that You would show me how to use them wisely and how to find ways to improve. Amen.

Mama Getting Weaker

Most assuredly, I say to you, he who hears My word and believes in Him who sent Me has everlasting life, and shall not come into judgement, but has passed from death into life.
John 5:24

For our visit with Mom after church, I'd taken some treats for the staff. I thought I'd leave the goodies in her room until someone could carry them down to the staff room, and then I planned to head off to the dining room to see Mom.

To my shock, Mom was still in her room. A PSW was gently trying to spoon some food into Mom's reluctant mouth while she was sitting up in bed. My alarm bells sounded.

What's wrong with Mom?" I asked.

"Your Mom didn't feel like going to the dining room for lunch, so I thought I'd bring it to her. She's just a little weak today."

"Oh, that is so sweet of you. Thank you," I said to the helpful girl.

Mom had her eyes closed when David and I came into her room, but when I spoke to her, she opened them.

"Oh hi," was about all Mom could muster.

I couldn't tell if she knew me or not.

"It's always nice to see you, Mom."

Hank and Janet popped in a bit later and after a while, Janet and I got to chatting. She told me something that she'd forgotten to share from her last visit with Mom. When Janet had arrived, apparently Mom said, "Oh it's good to see a clean face!" We figured she meant a "familiar face," but the word "clean" came out instead and we thought it was adorable. We couldn't help but love her.

Janet told me that the staff had called her a couple of days prior to our visit to say that Mom's moaning was more frequent, and she was getting very restless. They kept asking her if she was in pain. Mom didn't know. Just in case, they gave her a low-dose pain medication and she settled right down.

It happened again that morning. First the moaning and then the restlessness so they gave her some medication. Perhaps that was what made her sleepy. Pain meds knock me out, so maybe it was the same for her.

Once lunch was over, the PSW cleaned Mom up and helped her onto the bed. Mom didn't need much rocking. She was sound asleep in seconds, and she didn't open her eyes at all after that. We all finally left, content to know she was in good hands. It was getting harder to say goodbye, though.

Letting Go

Although we do not know the day or the hour, we do know Mama will soon be getting her wish to go to Heaven. It is always difficult to say goodbye, but especially when one does not know when that last goodbye will be. The important thing is to be there for our loved one or those we are responsible for, as we never know when it will be the last time.

Talking to God

Father. It is most difficult for me when I know that the end will be coming soon, but I have peace knowing that You know. Our days are numbered from birth and You see the entire picture all at once. This gives me great peace knowing I am in Your loving care. Amen.

Safe in the Arms of Jesus

Precious in the sight of the Lord
Is the death of His saints.
Psalm 116:15

Mom seemed to be doing well for a few weeks, so everyone encouraged me to go on our annual two-night "Girls Getaway" in Cobourg. Every year my friends and I book a cabin and spend a wonderful few days and nights together, catching up with each other; relaxing, eating, sharing our lives, and laughing out loud. I was sort of on the fence about going but then I felt at peace to go. So I did. The first day was wonderful. Such fun.

On the second evening, the text came from Janet. *Mom may not make it through the night.* I was full of anxiety and wondered how I would get home. Two of my dear friends decided to drive me toward the west. I had been in touch with David, and he was driving toward the east and, with the wonderful technology of cell phones, we met at a parking lot off the 401 in Toronto and I made the transfer.

David drove as fast as he safely could, and we arrived at Mom's room at 11:30 p.m. Janet had been with Mom all day and was most relieved to see us. I was thankful that Mom was still alive. She had one eye open when I arrived, as the pain medications were beginning to wear off.

I sat on her bed, stroked her hair, face, and arms and said, "Mama, Nancy is here. You can go home to Jesus now Mama. I love you Mama. I love you so much," over and over.

Finally, the nurse came and gave her two shots—one for pain and another to settle her down. Soon she drifted into a deep sleep.

Whenever Mom learned that a loved one or friend had died who loved Jesus, she would be jealous and ask when it would be her turn. Now it was a reality for my precious Mama. Although my tears fell, they were tears of a thankful heart because she was finally at perfect peace. I was so thankful that

I was there with Mama when she took her final breath. She always wanted to die in her sleep. She got her wish.

My sweet mama is now seeing Jesus face to face.

"Please give our daddy and sister, Jane, a hug from us Mama, for we miss them too, and look forward to the time when we're reunited with you all, once again."

Goodbye dear Mama, for now. It gives us great comfort to know that we shall meet again.

Bittersweet to Say Goodbye

Even though we may feel we are prepared to let go, it still is difficult. During these times, it helps if we have family or friends to surround us with love and comfort. It also causes us to be aware of the trauma others are experiencing and, hopefully, we can be there for them also when they need us.

Talking to God

Oh God. My heart is heavy. When a loved one is taken, it still hurts, no matter how old he or she is. I thank You, that because of the cross, I can be assured that my mother is with you. May I feel Your presence in the midst of all this sorrow. Amen.

Epilogue

Mom will always be known for her generosity in helping those in need. She made countless roast beef dinners with all the trimmings over the years. Anyone who had the honour of sitting at her table can attest that they'll never forget those meals. All who knew her, loved her, and the world is a little sadder without her.

Mom taught us how to love and trust God no matter what happened. She taught us to tithe at least ten percent and give joyfully to His work and God would look after us. It certainly has proven true and we're thankful for those lessons.

We know without a shadow of a doubt that our Mama is with the One she loved and served her whole life, and she is pain-free, young, and more joyful than ever. I like to imagine her being welcomed by Jesus, then by family and friends who had gone on before. That gives me great comfort.

Much to my surprise, I am taking Mom's death very hard. I truly thought I was prepared to let her go, for she was more than ready and longed to see Jesus. She was in pain during the last couple of weeks. Even though I would never ask her to come back, the reality that I have lost my precious Mama sends waves of hot tears. David comforts me, but they still come.

Although everything Mom did was behind the scenes, Heaven was fully aware of them all, and now she is reaping the rewards of her faithful service.

Our mother gave us detailed instructions for her funeral, and we had to laugh at these words we found written in block letters and underlined in red:

PLEASE DO NOT WASTE TIME BRAGGING ON ME BECAUSE IT IS ALL ABOUT GOD.

Even in death, Mom hated to be the centre of attention and we once again commented on how could it be possible that she raised three girls who were so comfortable on stage while she dreaded it?

This morning I made one last visit to Heritage House. I was emotional just driving down the dead-end street, parking in the lot, and seeing Mom's window, knowing she wasn't there. Another round of hot tears. I had decided to make three different treats for the staff, one last time. I placed the generous package containing my homemade marshmallow-rice squares, chocolate popcorn, chocolate bark, along with a typed thank-you note tucked into a bag on the nurses' desk.

Just before I left, the social director came over to thank me for the treats and the kind note and echoed what the others said over and over.

"We liked your mom very much and will miss her. We will also miss you and your family, too."

How very sweet. As I punched in the code to get out of the door for the last time, I cried. I inhaled deeply, walked to my car—and cried some more.

It hit me hard when I realized that David and I would not be visiting Mom after church anymore. But God is good, and He had planned ahead that our grandson Trenton would be baptized in the river that very afternoon. Matt and Sarah asked us to join them for a picnic lunch. It was a good time to witness another blessing. We watched joyfully, as Trenton publicly announced his faith in Jesus and was baptized. It was a most moving and delightful time. Later, we drove to their beautiful country home and saw the new lambs and all their other animals, the huge gardens and fruit trees, and all the work they'd done on the property. We ate delicious spaghetti on the patio, watched the kids play in the swimming pool, and played a rousing game of "May I?" God knew we needed to be refreshed. And we were.

My Example

Today we celebrate our precious mama's life. Give me courage, Lord. Take my hand.

I felt a heaviness when I woke up this morning, but then I realized that I do not have to go through this day alone. Not only do I have my wonderful family and friends surrounding me, I also have my dearest friend, Jesus, who promised to be as close as the mention of His name. He is always with me, but there are times I do not feel His presence, so I whisper, "Jesus," and I immediately know that He is real and is indeed walking right beside me, holding my hand. In fact, one of the songs we will be singing today is called, "He's My Dearest Friend." I honestly do not know what I would do without Him.

A good life goal is that God be honoured, for that is truly how Mom lived her life. Her legacy continues. I am who I am today, mostly because of the example our Mama gave us growing up. Her love and generosity will live on.

A Celebration of Life

We think she would have approved. All-in-all it was a memorable day, and we like to think that perhaps Mama *did* get to watch it from a heavenly vantage point.

We had many come up to us after and say things like, "This is exactly what I want when my time comes. I'm going to give detailed instructions to my family and make sure they follow it to the letter."

This made us feel happy. There was a great crowd (we estimated at least 180) and we each did our very best to honour our mother and to give glory to God; just as she requested.

It was our joy to sing a variety of songs, to have many scriptures read by the grandchildren, and to brag on our mom a little, even though she emphatically told us not to.

I loved what Angela (Hank and Janet's daughter) said before she and her siblings sang a beautiful song.

"Just as we parents like to hear people brag about our children, so must God love to hear us brag on one of His children, and today, we will brag about His daughter Flo."

Well put, Angela.

Mom's desire was that her family do the entire program, that the luncheon be substantial (not just sweets), for everything to be casual and light with plenty of singing, and that all the glory would go to the One she loved and served all her life. We tried very hard to do that.

(Left to Right) David, Nancy, Hank, and Janet sing at Mom's Celebration of life. June 27th, 2019

At the end of her notes and instructions for her funeral, she had written something that typified Mom.

"This looks like it will be a terrific time. I'm sorry that I'm going to miss it!"

We truly wanted God to be the centre of our celebration of a life well-lived, for He was the One who gave us all the gifts and talents and the venues to use them.

Way back in 1995, Mom began to write instructions for what she wanted this day to look like, and then a few years later added pages and pages yet again. We joked that if we would have followed every notation, we would have had to feed the people who attended not only lunch, but supper and breakfast the next day!

The Celebration of Life for our precious mama is complete.

On Dec. 18, 1964, after daddy died suddenly, my Mom was going through the pockets of his suit jacket to take to the funeral home and found a piece of paper with these words on it:

"Turn your eyes upon Jesus
Look full in His wonderful face.
And the things of earth
Will grow strangely dim
In the light of His glory and grace."[13]

We figured that daddy must have written the words down for us to learn. This was the song that my dear friend, Donna, was playing in the car when she and another friend and I were racing down the highway toward David, after I got the news that my Mama would not make it through the night.

Little did Daddy know how much that chorus would mean to us then, or how it would impact his middle daughter almost 55 years later when his wife, our Mama, was dying.

We, as caregivers, sometimes have our identity taken away when a loved one dies. Our life changes dramatically, and we feel a void. We also can feel a sense of relief that the one we

---

[13] Lyrics: Helen H. Lemmel, 1922. Public Domain

loved or were responsible for is finally at rest. Both are perfectly normal. It is important to grieve and let the tears flow when they surface. We all grieve differently, but the important thing is to let it out and not bottle it up. This will accelerate the healing. I encourage you all to turn *your* eyes upon Jesus.

Nancy

Acknowledgements

Thank you to my wonderful husband, and best friend, David, for walking beside me each step of the journey. You are my encourager, and you make me believe in myself when I am feeling low.

I could never have gone through this journey of caring for our mother without you, my sister, Janet. Together, we did our best to be with Mom as often as we could, didn't we? Even though we never knew what "mother" would greet us, we still did our best to stand tall and love Mom through it. It was good to walk together and lean on each other for support.

A huge thanks to my editor and publisher Glynis Belec. Your expertise in writing and publishing were appreciated and needed. We are a good team, aren't we?

My thanks to St. Jacobs Place and Heritage House. You all took good care of our mother and loved her as she dealt with dementia. Thank you for being so loving and kind, and oh, so patient.

And to my many friends who supported me and sent me perfectly timed words of encouragement, I am grateful. The journey would have been a lot tougher not having you there to cheer me on.

Finally, I thank you, God, for giving me the fortitude to plod on with hope in my heart and a smile on my face, even though there were days that I didn't think I could do it anymore. You knew otherwise and reminded me often.

David & Nancy

About the Author

Nancy has had a full life. She accepted Christ when she was five years old and enjoyed singing with her family from an early age. When she was 15, Nancy taught herself to be a ventriloquist. Her dream of being a wife and mother was fulfilled and now she enjoys being "Nana" to her five grandchildren.

Nancy was trained in theatre, and along with her husband, David, spent three and a half years full-time managing and acting in a travelling dinner theatre, raising funds for children in third world countries. She still enjoys singing, and writing on social media, and has a large following, including friends from all over the world because of her involvement with many missions and charities.

The idea for *When is Tomorrow?* came from her experiences dealing with her mother who suffered from dementia. Nancy kept a diary and realized that it would, one day, make a good devotional for caregivers.